Enid Yandell, Jean Loughborough, Laura Hayes

Three Girls In A Flat

Enid Yandell, Jean Loughborough, Laura Hayes

Three Girls In A Flat

ISBN/EAN: 9783742813701

Manufactured in Europe, USA, Canada, Australia, Japa

Cover: Foto ©Andreas Hilbeck / pixelio.de

Manufactured and distributed by brebook publishing software
(www.brebook.com)

Enid Yandell, Jean Loughborough, Laura Hayes

Three Girls In A Flat

THREE GIRLS IN A FLAT

Illustrated by....

HELEN M. ARMSTRONG
A. B. WENZELL
C. GRAHAM
TRUE WILLIAMS
J. H. VANDERPOEL
A. F. BROOKS
HUGH TALLANT
WALTER TALLANT OWEN

BY

ENID YANDELL, of Kentucky
JEAN LOUGHBOROUGH, of Arkansas
LAURA HAYES, of Illinois

PRESS OF
KNIGHT, LEONARD & CO
CHICAGO.

TO

That noble body of women which is acting as advance-

guard to the great army of the unrecognized

in its onward march toward liberty

and equality —

THE BOARD OF LADY MANAGERS

of the

WORLD'S COLUMBIAN EXPOSITION.

PREFACE

We beg to assure our readers that we do not consider this little book in any way a literary effort.

It is a simple story which really wrote itself, and it is with great modesty and hesitation that we cast it upon the sea of public opinion.

THREE GIRLS IN A FLAT

OVR FLAT

CHAPTER I.

IT was growing late and Gene and the Duke were dressing for dinner in the great dreary room in the boarding-house owned in partnership by the girls. The Duke had let down the masses of her blue-black hair, while Gene was engaged in untangling a refractory shoe-lace, when a little knock came at the door, and a moment after Marjorie entered. She looked pale and worn, and as the girls looked up with a welcoming smile, Gene said, " What's the matter, dear, you look so tired to-night." Marjorie threw herself into a chair, and said, " It's the flat again. I have just had a note from Mrs. Black, saying that owing to a sudden change in her husband's business they have been called to New York, and now that white elephant is on my hands once more." " What *is* the flat? " asked the Duke, with interest. " Why, don't you know? " said Gene; " it has been the bane of Marjorie's existence for the last two years, for it contains all of her mother's furniture which she does not want to store, and the people to whom she rents it are always getting sick or leaving town, or for some reason or other giving it up, so it is on her hands again." " Where is it? " demanded the Duke. " Why, it is only two blocks down the street and in a very pleasant neighborhood, and for my

9

part I wish *we* lived in it instead of in this dreary old boarding-house, where we can't get a thing to eat if we are not on
time for meals." "Why not go to housekeeping?" cried
the Duke, and the same thought came like a flash to all
three, and then and there, regardless of the approaching
dinner, they sat down to discuss eagerly the ways and
means of accomplishing their object.

Two weeks later the girls came home to their own
hearth and fireside. They had brought two friends with

them to spend the night, and when the five girls gathered
around the snowy table, with its bunch of flowers, in the
pretty dining-room, with its sideboard full of the beautiful
old-fashioned silver that had belonged to Marjorie's
mother, it was with the happiest feeling they had all known
for many a day. The neat little maid who had worked in

"WHAT'S THE MATTER, DEAR? YOU LOOK SO TIRED."

the flat for the preceding occupants had stayed with them,
and no one would ever have guessed from the way in
which she served the dinner that it had all been cooked by
herself in the little kitchen beyond.

It was not a very large suite of rooms—just seven, but
they were comfortable and very light, having side windows
that overlooked a field of waving grass, an unusual thing
in the city.

(The Duke, who was standing at the dining-room window when I first read this chapter aloud, interrupted to say
that I had forgotten to mention the adornments of the
field, which consisted of a rusty stove, two battered silk

hats, an old tin bath-tub with a hole in it, ten tomato cans and the janitor's six children.)

There was the parlor with its cheerful fire-light, the little library with its pictures, copies, for the most part, of famous paintings, and its rows of books in their leather-

trimmed cases, and the dining-room and kitchen; then there was a room apiece for the girls; but I must not forget to mention one of the most important features of all—the hammock in the library. This great soft web of blue and white which swung in the half-darkness and yet gave a glimpse of the ruddy hearth in the parlor beyond, was a

favorite resort of one, two and sometimes three tired girls,
who could escape through the library door to their own
rooms at the importunate ring of the door-bell.

THE JANITOR'S CHILDREN.

There had been one subject that had nearly wrecked
their plans of housekeeping, and this had been the question of a chaperone, which they had discussed from every
standpoint and with much feeling, for Gene had insisted
upon having one, although, as she admitted, it would spoil
much of their comfort, as there was no room for her in the
flat. But even Gene's conservative ideas were finally
changed by the two obstacles which presented themselves.
The first was the impossibility of finding a chaperone that
they liked (as they were strangers in the city and did not
know who to call upon), and the second was the necessity of
supporting her should they be able to find one. It was the
latter point that settled the question finally, as the girls felt

that they could not add to their expenses so materially, and they could hardly ask their chaperone to board with them.

There had been no changes to make, except the purchase

of two new rugs, which the girls had taken as much pleasure in selecting as if they had been buying the outfit for a stately mansion. The week before moving in, Virginia had run over to the flat one morning to look about and see what there was to be done and to measure the parlor floor for the first new rug. She had left the door accidentally open, and was on her knees with tape measure in hand when she was startled by a voice behind her saying inquiringly, " Miss Fairfax ? " She turned in some surprise at hearing her name, for the girls had only been to their new home once, and that after dark, and no one could possibly have known of their coming.

Before her stood a stout woman with rather an elegant figure and a tired and careworn look. She was dressed in a plain skirt covered by a large apron, and what Gene afterward described as a "grey and melancholy waist" and

her appearance betokened respectable shabbiness. Her eyes, which must have been beautiful before sorrow had dimmed their lustre, rolled curiously about the room, as she stood watching Gene. Her soft, gray hair was banded away from a low brow, her hands were aristocratic and well kept, and her voice was soft and cultured as she spoke. Gene was beginning to wonder if she had dropped out of the sky, as she had not heard her enter, when she explained her appearance by saying "I am your neighbor,

Mrs. Brown. I saw you come in and thought I would run down and have a chat with you this morning." Then interrupting herself, as she saw Gene's occupation, "What, are you going to get new rugs? Now I call that very shabby of you, when we live just overhead and our carpets are so old and worn." Gene tried to murmur some apology

COPIES OF FAMOUS PAINTINGS.

for having even thought of buying anything new without consulting our neighbors, when Mrs. Brown rambled on: "Are you any relation to old Governor Fairfax of Virginia? What, not his granddaughter? I am delighted to hear it, and I might have known it from that straight nose of yours. Blood will tell every time, I say. Now you must meet my husband's sister, Mrs. Jackson, who lives with me. She belongs to the old Jackson family of Virginia, and they lived right in the next county to the Fairfaxes in the old Dominion State," and Mrs. Brown chattered on in the most interesting but interminable manner, until Gene, who was half vexed with the delay, could not help being amused at the perfect friendliness and freedom with which her new acquaintance regaled her with family history. As soon as she discovered that Gene was one of *the* Fairfax family, she took her into her confidence, and before she left, Virginia was in possession of the facts that Mrs. Brown had been a reigning belle at Baltimore in her youth, and had wedded at an early age a brilliant young physician who had once figured prominently before the people of the United States through an Arctic expedition, though this marriage, as she candidly admitted, had been but an incident in her career. By it, however, she had reached a most enviable position, and had been for several years petted and

ARIADNE.

idolized by a large circle of friends and admirers. After Dr. Jackson's death, which left her nearly penniless, she had returned to Baltimore, where she lived in great retirement, until one day, having been persuaded to go to a dinner, (where, as we subsequently learned from Mrs. Jackson, she was charming in a simple toilet of white muslin and blue ribbons) she met her fate in handsome Andrew Brown, who in return, fell instantly in love with her and they were married soon after.

Many happy years of wedded life followed, when Mr. Brown, who was one of the finest men in the world, died of a fever, leaving her with a large family of children to educate. She had preferred to leave Baltimore when she was obliged to sell her home, and after trying several cities had finally settled in Chicago. All this she told Virginia, and with perfect candor stated the exact amount of her present income, which was not large, the number of frocks Ariadne wore out each year, and the size of their last month's butcher bill (which they had forgotten to pay).

When Gene came home and told us about her interview with our neighbor and mentioned the number in the family, we felt our first misgiving as to our new home.

JEAN PAUL.

There was Mrs. Brown, her sister Mrs. Jackson; Ariadne, aged twenty; Jean Paul, fourteen; Lycurgus, twelve; Thomas Jefferson, ten; and little Philander, popularly known as Phil., aged two; and all of these in a seven-room flat which just furnished us three girls with a bedroom each and left none to spare.

We had interviewed the landlord and succeeded in getting his promise to put new papering in the dining-room, we had ordered the rugs, and were getting the ruffled muslin curtains made, expecting to move on the following Tuesday, when one morning brought a note from Mrs. Brown.

"Dear Miss Fairfax," it ran, "I write to tell you of my terrible dilemma, and to beg that if possible you will aid me to escape. Ariadne was invited so many places last winter, that she must give a little party in return, and Lycurgus wants to entertain his classmates for an evening, and would you oblige us by letting us have the use of your

flat next Thursday and Friday? Our piano is in your dining-room, and it would be so nice for the children to dance
in there. I ask you to do us this kindness, knowing that
you cannot be cruel enough to refuse, when I tell you that
the invitations are already out." And the note concluded
by begging the pleasure of our company for Thursday
evening following.

We had a long and earnest debate over this remarkable
communication, and the Duke vowed with a strange and
terrible vow that we should not allow ourselves
to be thus imposed upon; and that we could
not postpone our moving for three days at the
request of a mere stranger; but the upshot of it
all was that Virginia wrote a courteous note, giving Mrs. Brown the necessary permission, and
promising to attend if possible.

LYCURGUS.

I will not go into details and explain how
Gene did go to the party, nor will I tell of the
anguish of mind with which she joined the
crowd in our dear little flat, who were dancing
the wax off the newly polished floors, and elbowing the art
paper that had just been placed upon the dining-room wall.
But this was not the worst: for many weeks afterwards we
kept meeting friends on the street who regretted so much
that they could not come to "our party" that Thursday
night, and we learned to our dismay that the invitations
had been given out in our joint names.

We had not been settled long before we had become
acquainted with the entire family, and a more happy, enter
taining, shiftless, pleasant set of people it was never our
good fortune to meet. There was only one drawback, and
that was that there were so many of them. It was all very

well to have Ariadne with her quiet manners and her pale
face come in and spend the evening, or to hear a knock at
the door and opening it find
three little kittens that mischievous Tom had deserted
on our threshold; and it was
pleasant, too, to have Mrs.
Jackson come in
with her reddish wig
and Spanish lace
mantilla to tell us
the tales of bygone
days—but it was al-
ways someone. Ly-

curgus would surprise us by dangling strange and unexpected things down the shaft into our bath-room, or little

Philander would come in with his toys to stay as long as
he was allowed; but the one who came most frequently was
Mrs. Brown herself, who never could stay very long, but
who always appeared at a most unexpected moment. We
all took it good-naturedly enough except the Duke who
rather rebelled, though she did not say much.

One evening, however, she had a caller, and had been
interrupted two or three times by Mrs. Brown's knocking
at the front door. She had opened it each time very politely and asked her to come in, but at last her patience was
exhausted, and when the fourth knock came she did not
move. Mrs. Brown knocked and called once or twice, for
she knew that the Duke was inside; but that stubborn
young woman refused to answer, though Cousin John could
hardly restrain his laughter. Mrs. Brown, however, was
not to be outdone in that way. It was but the work of a
moment to go to her kitchen, down the back stairs, in our
back door, and back into the parlor, which she entered exclaiming triumphantly: " You see you can't keep me out,
Miss Wendell," and the poor Duke was overcome with
shame and confusion, especially as Mrs. Brown carried
with her a plate of delicious home-made candy that Ariadne had made that afternoon.

They borrowed everything we had, from hats through
to shoe-blacking, but the climax was reached one Sunday
morning when Mrs. Brown came to the front door and
asked if she might take our frying pan. Virginia, who had
answered the knock, said " Why of course Mrs. Brown, if
we have one, and I suppose that we have; I'll ring and tell
Katie to bring it to you." "Oh, no," said Mrs. Brown,
" I'll just run back into the kitchen and get it myself "; but
Virginia planted herself in the way, for she knew that the

girls were still at breakfast, and that Mr. Middleton had just come with his Sunday morning flowers, and she did not care to have our neighbors prying into our affairs. Now Gene has a great deal of dignity, and it would take some courage to pass her with that determined look in her

eyes, but Mrs. Brown neither looked nor stopped until she reached the kitchen. Marjorie had gone to her room for something, so as Mrs. Brown passed through the dining-room she caught a glimpse of the Duke and Mr. Middleton, who were talking together. As she came back she held the frying-pan up beside her face like a huge lorgnette, saying: " Never mind, young people I won't look at you," which made the Duke perfectly furious, although she

did not in the least consider Mr. Middleton her particular
prey.

But if they borrowed of us they were equally willing to
lend, as was proven the night that Marjorie was going
to the Charity Ball. Mrs. Brown had heard her say that
she did not have anything to wear, so at eight o'clock that
evening her customary knock was heard and she entered
with a great armful of old-fashioned flounces of black lace
and with a most exquisite point lace shawl, which she
insisted upon draping about Marjorie until she saw on the
bed the pretty tulle gown of pale blue, with its wreaths
of rosebuds, which the girls had made that day, when she
desisted.

All the Brown family were exceedingly strict about
chaperones. They frankly confessed that they were
shocked when the girls went to the opera or to the theatre
with young men, even though the cavaliers in question
were cousins or old, old friends. Poor Ariadne in consequence was deprived of many an innocent pleasure, for
it was quite impossible to chat with callers at home when
she knew that all the family were playing whist in the next
room within hearing and would comment on the conversation at breakfast the next day, or when wicked Tom would
come dancing by the hall door in his night dress, making
faces of fiendish delight as he saw her torment.

But it was too much for our gravity when Mrs. Brown
told us of an incident that happened one day when Mrs.
Jackson wanted Dr. Gordon to look at her throat which
had been troubling her. Now Dr. Gordon is an extremely
pleasant young fellow, good looking as Apollo and yet
entirely wanting in the conceit that makes handsome men
usually odious. He has the highest professional and social

standing, and moreover, he was a warm friend of the Brown family. The two ladies went over to the drug-store on the corner, where they sat in state while they sent the clerk up stairs to call the young doctor down, for as

HTALLANT

THE BRIDE.

Mrs. Brown afterwards confessed, "it would have been *so* improper for dear Mrs. Jackson to have gone to his office." Mrs. Jackson's conscious look when Mrs. Brown made this remark showed that despite her eighty-nine years, she con-curred in this opinion.

But despite their little peculiarities, we enjoyed the Browns. Their comings and goings were a source of infinite distraction, and we should have missed them sorely had they moved away.

Below us lived a young married couple who were evidently from the country. The bride was both young and pretty, though as Mrs. Brown said, she had "no style;" but it was the occupation of her life to prevent the neighbors from making the discovery that she kept no servant. Instead of emptying her ashes in the chute which would have necessitated her appearance in the back hall, she saved them up for several days, and then after dark carried them cautiously down her stairs into the cellar, and taking off the lids filled all the laundry stoves. She had another little peculiarity—so Katie told us—of throwing her dishwater out of the window into the clean, stone-paved court where the handmaids of the flats usually congregated in the evening with their beaux. One of the excitements of the back hall was the warfare waged against the lower flat by all the servants, who were assisted in the crusade by their firm friends, the butchers and milkmen.

Just across the hall on the same floor, dwelt some neighbors of a very different stamp. Here, in great retirement, lived a well-known general and his charming family. His wife had been the widow of a prominent politician who had figured as candidate in a notable presidential campaign, and her grace and beauty had given her an almost national reputation. As her husband's health was delicate, she went but little into society, but busied herself with her duties to her children and her church, to which she was devoted. Her daughters had inherited her beauty, and no amount of seclusion could keep the glances of admiration from noting the great black eyes of the elder, or the heavy chestnut braids and glowing cheeks of the younger. Edith was our especial friend, and it was Gene's delight to coax her into a literary or scientific dicussion and see her cheeks kindle and her eyes flash with the inherited power of oratory when she became interested in her subject.

Taking it altogether, we felt that we were particularly happy in our neighbors.

CHAPTER II.

PARIS.

HEN dinner was over the girls usually gathered round the cannel fire in the parlor for a chat, and so it happened on a certain stormy evening in October. Outside the wind howled up and down the deserted street, but within it was the picture of comfort and good cheer. It was too early for callers, and the Duke had thrown herself full length into her favorite chair, while Gene sat in the lamplight trimming her hat for the fourth time that week. "Won't you get us your diary, Marjorie, and read us a little about your trip abroad?" asked the Duke. "You have promised so many times to do it." "Why, of course," and Marjorie left the room returning in a few minutes with her black leather book, while the girls settled themselves to listen.

She opened at random and commenced to read "June 29, 1891. When we first arrived in Paris Mrs. Palmer received a call from Mr. Theodore Stanton, who is the correspondent for the Associated Press, and who has resided in Paris for over twelve years. He was an extremely handsome and amiable man with bright color in his face and in his golden beard, and in the deep blue of his eyes. Perhaps to me he seemed especially good to look at because he was so American in his speech and dress, and in the cheerful enthusiasm that pervaded his manner. It was a comfort to meet a real countryman after the many insipid imitations we had seen in the streets of London, who were ashamed to be American, and could not be successfully English, and who, as a result, were a type of nothing under the sun.

But to return to Mr. Stanton. He began to ask at once

about the part women were to take in the World's Fair, and handled the woman question with an ease and fearlessness that could only have come from deep conviction or early training. I afterwards discovered that it was both, as he was the son of that much-loved and revered woman, Elizabeth Cady Stanton. When he learned that Mrs. Palmer was to be in the city only a few days, he seemed much disappointed, as he said he wanted her to meet some of the leaders in women's work in Paris, especially Madame De Morsier, who had taken such a prominent part in the Paris Exposition of '89. Mrs. Palmer explained that she would return in a few weeks, when she would be very happy to meet the French ladies, and so it was arranged that Mme. De Morsier should call before her departure and make the preliminary arrangements. She came a few days later, and it was a comfort to find that she really spoke excellent English, though with a quaint little accent. She had a sweet, intelligent face, a matronly

figure and a very cordial manner, and she proved to be a valuable acquaintance, for she came to see Mrs. Palmer many times, arranged a meeting with M. Guyot and others, and took such a friendly interest from the first in the part women were to take in the coming Exposition, that her example proved contagious.

"Whether or not there were other agencies at work I never fully understood, but as soon as she returned from her two-weeks' trip to Vienna, Mrs. Palmer was asked in the most delicate and diplomatic way if she would consent to receive a few of the French women who were interested in her work, and if so what place would be convenient. She named the following Wednesday, and said she would see them in her salon at the Grand Hotel.

"We did not know exactly who would come, but Madame De Morsier thought there would probably be about twelve people, and she promised to be on hand early and introduce the first comers.

"Wednesday proved a clear and cloudless day, one of the warmest we had encountered since leaving home, and after

looking over her mail, as usual, and telling me how to dispose of it, Mrs. Palmer began to consider the afternoon.

"She had an engagement for luncheon, and so the arrangements were left to me, to my great delight, for I thoroughly enjoy anything that savors of housekeeping, for which, probably because I have never tried it, I have always felt that I had a peculiar aptitude.

"First I sent for the steward and instructed him as to the serving of the coffee, tea and chocolate ; then I went to Boissiers myself and ordered the confections and the delicious little cakes for which that establishment is so justly famous, and finally to the flower market on the corner by the Madeleine, where I bought to my heart's content, taking a whole mass in my "voiture," while two stout men ran down the boulevard beside it, each with a load on his back. I worked with a will and I must say the rooms looked charming, for I had often decorated them before

on flower-market day for the mere pleasure it gave us all
to see them looking so pretty.

"The salon proper was a very large apartment on the
first floor above the street, and in the corner of the Avenue
de l'Opera and the Boulevard; and there were many lace-
draped windows opening full length, in the French way, on
to a large balcony, so that it was but the work of a
moment to step out into the June day and be right over
the gayest corner of the gayest street in Paris, with its
multitudes of little tables, and its beautifully dressed
promenaders. Within the room was gorgeous. The walls
were hung with red brocade, and the wood work was of
white enamel, while from the great candelabra placed here
and there, and hanging from the ceiling, depended hundreds of oak leaves of shining crystal.

"The flowers were very simply arranged, but there was a
huge Japanese punch-bowl full of what Min called "blue
carnations " on the center-table, while the tall bronze jars
on the marble cabinets between the windows blossomed
over into snowy lilies, that repeated themselves in the
mirrors behind them in endless nodding reflections.
Through the open doors leading into the next salon could
be seen the rose-crowned table with its dainty appointments.

"The first to arrive was Madame de Morsier, according to
her promise ; then followed M. and Madame Jules Siegfried,
and more people came singly and in groups until every
chair in the room was taken and we were obliged to send
for more. After all were seated and chatting comfortably
to their neighbors in the cheerful French fashion, Madame
de Morsier rose, and in simple and dignified language explained the part women were to take in the World's Co-

lumbian Exposition. She spoke in
French, and as she talked I glanced
around at her audience.

"There must have been
forty people in the room,
some of them gentlemen,
and as we afterwards
learned,
prominent
members of
the Cham-

ber of Deputies, which corresponds to
our Congress.

"Just behind her sat a distinguished
line of women. First, Madame Guyot,

the bright and progressive wife of M. Yves Guyot, who was at that time minister of public works, and a member of the Cabinet. She was accompanied by her daughter, who was charming, and a perfect type of the *jeune fille*, sweet and modest as a blush-rose bud. Then Madame Siegfried, Madame Bogelot, who has done such magnificent work for women in the dreadful prison of St. Lazare, and our own Mrs. Logan, whose earnest black eyes, under the halo of snowy hair, watched every movement of the speaker with great interest. Mrs. Logan was accom-

panied by her son and his wife, who were both very pleasant and entertaining. Next to them sat Mrs. Harrison and Mrs. McKee, who were visiting Mrs. Whitelaw Reid, and who made so many friends abroad wherever they appeared. One of the Americans residing in Paris spoke of them as "our American Princesses," and the name soon became popular. Next to them sat Mrs. Palmer and by her side Miss Hallowell, who is one of the most widely acquainted of our countrywomen in Paris. Her opinion is sought and respected on everything connected with art, and she has a warm personal acquaintance with all the painters and sculptors who constitute the charmed inner circle in the famous art life of the gay capital. Last of all was Mrs. May Wright Sewell of Indianapolis, who was the American delegate to the Exposition Congress of Women in Paris in 1889, and who consequently has an acquaintance with numbers of prominent workers among the French people.

"The Americans had been invited by Mrs. Palmer, and as I looked around the room I could not restrain a feeling of pride, for I knew our ladies did not suffer in comparison.

"Madame de Morsier spoke of the interest felt by every one in Paris in the Exposition, and cited in instance of it, that M. Jules Simon had expressed to her his willingness to be present on this occasion. It is difficult to explain in English just how she said it, but we all gathered that he had sent the message as a token of friendliness and good will, and without the actual intention of coming. When she told this I heard little murmurs,  and saw the approving nods around the room, for M. Simon is probably more respected and loved than any statesman in France at the present day. He has been honored by a Senatorship for life, and although he is now quite an old man, he still retains unimpaired his wonderful faculties.

" Madame de Morsier had found no difficulty in describing the moral and philanthropic aims of the Board of Lady Managers, but when she came to the more practical part of the undertaking and tried to tell about the Woman's Building, it was evident that she, like so many others, was confused by the words 'separate' and 'special' exhibits.

M. Siegfried interrupted her with a question, and Mrs. Palmer leaned forward, and tried to tell her in a few low words how to reply. Madame de Morsier was about to proceed, when M. Siegfried politely asked, 'Will not Mrs. Palmer explain this point to us herself?' She rose smiling, and said, 'I beg that you will excuse me, as my French is somewhat limited, and Madame de Morsier will tell you about it much better than I could possibly do.' 'No, no, no,' came from all parts of the room; 'Let us hear Mrs. Palmer, she speaks French very well,' etc., etc., and amid the chorus of echoing voices she was obliged to rise again.

"I shall never forget how she looked as she stood in the middle of the large salon, explaining to these distinguished French people in their own language the difficult points that would require an unusual vocabulary and a judicious choice of words in one's own tongue. Sometimes she was at a loss for a moment, and then she would stop and appeal to M. Siegfried, or change her way of phrasing, for it was quite a different thing to talking the ordinary French of shop or drawing-room, which she speaks with fluency. She never for an instant lost the perfect self-poise and charming dignity that lent an added impressiveness to her every word.

"As I saw the interest deepening on every face, turned to this slender young woman, and noted the deferential attention given, not to her beauty or her position, or to the grace of her manner, but to her wonderful intelligence, and to the clear reasoning that dominated her hesitating speech, I felt a strange sense of emotion. Miss Hallowell leaned over to me and whispered, 'I never expected to see such a sight as this,' and I noticed the moisture in her eyes.

"After Mrs. Palmer had explained the doubtful point, several of the gentlemen asked questions, to all of which she replied with perfect readiness, and then the conversation became general. M. Siegfried, who is a tall, imposing man, with a bushy, red beard, talked very sensibly on the ways and means of forming a new committee which was to co-operate with the Board of Lady Managers in France, and I may say that he and his interesting wife from that moment did everything in their power to insure the success of the new idea.

"After several other people had spoken I noticed a little stir near the door, and the man at the entrance announced in a loud voice—'M. Jules Simon.' As the great man entered every body rose to his feet, and Mrs. Palmer walked far across the room to welcome him. It was delightful to see the deference with which he was treated. No one seemed to think it was at all unusual to go over the entire situation again as if nothing had been said before; and when he rose and made a few amiable remarks in his thin, quavering voice, it was touching to see the pleasure and enthusiasm with which they were received. His unexpected coming gave the finishing touch to a very successful day, and after this the meeting became entirely informal and many confidential groups could be seen chatting over a cup of tea.

"Soon after this, and without her own seeking, Mrs. Palmer had an audience with several important people, including Madame Carnot, who complimented her by presenting her with the President's box at the Comédie Française, and it was on the Saturday following the reception that the members of the World's Fair Committee in the Chamber of Deputies expressed their willingness to have women appointed officially to co-operate with the Board of Lady Managers, in collecting the exhibit of women's work for the Exposition."

As Marjorie finished reading the door bell rang, and without time for comment the girls hastily flew to their rooms to prepare for the evening's campaign, for it was Friday, and many callers were expected.

CHAPTER III.

FRIDAY EVENINGS.

N the parlor we gathered in our best attire, for we had found a reception evening at last, when we were all at home. The new jardinière, which Marjorie had made out of an old box and some Lincrusta Walton, was filled with tall chrysanthemums, our best cups and souvenir spoons were arranged on the little Turkish table, and last of all we lighted the lamp under the brass tea-kettle, and then seated ourselves to "await the rush," as the Duke said. We were watching the smoke coming in volumes from the throat of the tea-kettle, when a gentle knock was heard at the door.

Marjorie rose with a most winning smile to greet—Mrs. Brown!

"Ah, good evening," said our irrepressible neighbor; "Expecting company?" and she glanced at Gene's white gown!

"Oh, no; we always dress this way in the evening."

And the Duke, who had not forgotten the molasses candy episode, looked severely at Mrs. Brown.

"Why, I think I'll stay and take a cup of tea with you. Looks cozy, doesn't it?"

And the good woman with a serene smile settled herself comfortably before the fire, put her feet upon the newly polished brass fender and sipped our fragrant Bohea, which Marjorie offered her, I must confess a little grudgingly.

"You know Mrs. Jackson always says that I am pretty lucky, and I begin to think I am," she continued, heedless of the fact that we were not any of us particularly cordial. "Did I tell you, Miss Fairfax, that I was going to apply to our landlord for a new Pasteur filter? Well, while I was making an application I wrote down a list of things : a new filter, a stained-glass window in the bathroom and wire screens for the windows, and will you believe me when I tell you that he sent them all ? I was more surprised than any one else."

"I don't understand that at all, Mrs. Brown," said Marjorie, putting her teacup down on the table with emphasis.

"Never mind, my dear, I do. My nephew James is on the editorial staff of the *Herald*, and he could so easily mention that the St. Julien Flats are managed well—or otherwise, you know."

"But, Mrs. Brown, think of the injustice of it. Here we have repeatedly asked to have Katie's room calcimined, and Mr. Thompkins has paid no attention to us, and we finally had it done at our own expense."

"I am very sorry indeed, my dear, but I cannot help it. I will have to drown my sorrow in another cup of your delicious tea," she answered, laughingly.

Virginia, who saw that Mrs. Brown was a fixture, resorted to a little strategy, as we did not desire her to be one of our reception committee.

"Mrs. Brown, you must come out and see Katie's room. We told her to choose any color she liked for her walls, and to our horror she chose an intense rose color, which does not go well with her auburn hair."

Mrs. Brown arose, and we followed her to the kitchen hoping that she would go on upstairs to her own flat. Katie's room amused her very much, with its rose-colored walls, and the box in one corner covered with turkey-red calico and some coarse white lace, while the same lace hung from the windows and was looped back with red ribbon bows. As we were talking the bell rang, and little Mary went to open the door. We breathed a sigh of relief as Mrs. Brown said:

"Oh, I must go now—but who do you suppose it is, girls? I believe I'll just peep through the back parlor door," and before we could remonstrate with her, she had walked out into the hall, followed by Virginia, who looked calm but resigned.

"Here, let me see the name," and our worthy neighbor seized the card from little Mary's tray.

"E. T. Barker! Why, my dear, he was one of Dr. Jackson's most devoted friends." And before we fully realized it Mrs. Brown had glided into the parlor and was greeting effusively Major Barker, late Minister to Turkey, and a charming man.

There was no help for it, so we followed her and acted as assistants, while she played hostess. The parlor was soon filled and we were having a very jolly time, for if there is one thing for which Mrs. Brown is famous, it is entertaining, and she does it royally.

"Now do take another cup of tea, Major—and you say you brought a cook from the Orient?"

"I did, my dear madam, and in honor of the arrival of my foreign *chef*, I invited a number of friends to dinner, and what do you suppose he gave us? Upon my word and honor, all we had were carrots and molasses candy mixed!"

Just here little Mary announced Colonel Rogers, and through the curtain we caught a glimpse of a tall, uncouth looking man, with a broad slouch hat, which he hung with a flounce on our little hat-rack, almost covering it.

The announcement was quickly followed by the gentleman himself, who came into the room in a breezy manner which took us all by storm. He strode up to the Duke and seized her by both hands.

He was at least six feet tall and fleshy in proportion, while his face was round and bespoke good nature. His hair stood straight up all over his head, and looked as if there was no treaty of reciprocity between it and the brush.

The Duke introduced him as Colonel Rogers, of Kentucky, and after cordially shaking each guest by the hand, he seated himself comfortably in our best rocking-chair and beamed amiably on the assembled company. Under his broad, turn-down collar was a thin black ribbon, tied in a straggling bow, which, before the evening was over, had worked itself around under his left ear. His whiskers formed an aggressive halo around his face, and his clothes were large and roomy, and were evidently made for comfort. His vest was fastened at the top and bottom, but the intervening space was guiltless of buttons.

Pulling his chair towards Major Barker, he carelessly crossed his feet, and I noticed that over one of his large shoes dangled a white string.

"Well, Miss Duke, I tried to send my card up in that whistle, but I couldn't make it work," and the Colonel threw back his head and laughed heartily.

"I tell you, you all have so many new fangled notions here in Chicago that I wouldn't be surprised at anything. Major, are you a native?"

Major Barker, seeing that he had an entertaining specimen near him, answered heartily:

"Yes, Colonel, I am. And your home is in Kentucky, I presume?"

"Yes, I am a native Kentuckian, born and raised in the Green River country. I've represented my county twice in the Legislature, and have been a candidate three times for Circuit Jedge."

His not having been elected cut no figure with the Colonel, as the fact of being a candidate, though three times unsuccessful, was honor enough for him.

"Now, this cane was presented to me in '8o by the Committee on Agriculture, of which I had the honor of being Chairman."

And the Colonel leaned out and took from the hat-rack in our little hall an unwieldly cane with a massive gold head.

"Made the finest speech in my life when that cane was given to me—fairly bro't down the house, and Jedge Emerson told me afterwards that he tho't it was the effort of my life."

"Talking of oratory, Colonel, do you know Colonel McKenzie?"

"What, Quinine Jim? Best friend I've got in the world. Why, he was raised next do' to me in the Green River country, and there ain't no finer man between Pennyrile and the Purchase than that very Jim McKenzie."

Just here I want to say that the State of Kentucky is divided into four sections—the "Mountains," the "Bluegrass," the "Pennyroyal" and the "Purchase," the district between the last two sections being the Colonel's home.

"And if it hadn't been for me," Colonel Rogers continued pompously, "I don't think Jim ever would have been in Congress; for the first time he run it was pretty shaky, but the members of our section of the Congressional Deestrict just took off our coats and wheeled our counties into line for Jim, and we've been proud of it ever sence. I tell you, he is the tallest talker in the State, and can talk all around any one of them Congressmen."

And at the recollection of his friend's political prowess, the Colonel put his hand affectionately on Major Barker's knee.

"Why do you call him Quinine Jim?"

"Because he made the famous speech in Congress to take the tariff off quinine so we could buy it cheap, for in our deestrict there are so many swamps that we buy quinine by the pound, and then we shake our teeth out."

And the Colonel gave another of his laughs at this remark, demonstrating to the entire company that the best of his teeth had been shaken out years ago.

" Yes, Jim McKenzie has fixed things now so that a poor man can afford to have a chill now and then."

We girls silently sipped our tea, for the conversation was absorbed by Colonel Rogers, and our guests formed an interested group around him, while he was in his element, being the center of attraction.

Mrs. Brown was having the best time of anybody, and many a furtive glance did the Colonel cast at her comely, matronly figure, as he recited his experiences. She was not a beautiful Desdemona, but she evidently pleased this modern Othello, and the thought of the six little motherless Browns across the way never entered her head.

We were just about to accompany Colonel Rogers through another political campaign, when little Mary approached Mrs. Brown and whispered excitedly :

" Please, ma'am, Miss Ariadne thinks Philander has swallowed something, and we are afraid it is a tack."

The Colonel, who had heard it, immediately arose and looked more agitated than the mother, and with all the elegance resulting from the polishing influence of two terms in the Kentucky Legislature, said : "Allow me to serve you, my dear madam ; can I go for a doctor ?"

" Oh, no, not at all," Mrs. Brown answered nonchalantly. "I don't mind his swallowing tacks, if he will only let nickels and dimes alone. Why, he has quite depleted my purse, and the number of buttons he has disposed of is something astonishing."

And with many courtesies the worthy lady made her adieu—reluctantly, I must admit—while the Colonel, with

much deliberate ceremony, handed her out of the door,
Mrs. Brown, with quiet elegance mincing out:—for Philander
could swallow tacks, nickels, dimes and the United States
mint, but his mother must not forget her deportment.

" Ah, good-night, Colonel, I trust I shall hear more of
your exceedingly interesting experiences at another time."

" But, my dear madam, allow me to see you to your
own door."

" Girls, I can't miss that fun," and the Duke followed
them out into the hall. She afterwards told us that Ariadne
was holding the door open for her mother, and from the
stairs she caught sight of the bedroom where the five small
Browns were domiciled. She said that Philander was in
the middle of the bed gasping for breath, and about him
were as many small brothers as could be accommodated
with a sight of his sufferings, while the boys who could not
get near enough were consoling themselves by tumbling
somersaults over the foot of the adjoining bed, all five being in various stages of undress.

When the Colonel returned he began a lengthy reminis-
cence upon the times that his sons had gotten into similar
difficulties, and the remedies that he had used, ending with
the astonishing announcement that the best thing as far as
he knew for everything was a good, stout toddy.

" By the way, Major, did you ever drink any of the mint
juleps made after Colonel Stoddard Johnson's recipe? You
haven't ! Well, I tell you, if you ever come out to old
Kaintuck, I'll give you such another julep as you never
tasted in all your life before."

We began to fear that our tea had fallen dead against
the Colonel's lurid palate. But nevertheless he waxed eloquent and poetic as he described the mint-bed in his own

back yard at home, declaring that the moon only shone at its best in old Kentucky, when the mocking-birds were singing in the chinquepin trees, and we began to think that Mrs. Brown's influence and a cup of tea had certainly inspired him.

"Very fine woman, that Mrs. Brown," said the Colonel, as he gave a masterly stroke to his aggressive whiskers. "Er—ah—a widow?"

"Yes," said Marjorie, "she is the widow of the late Judge Brown, who was an old Baltimorean, though he fought on the Northern side in the war."

"You don't say so! She can't be the widow of Andrew Brown? What! She is? Why, I remember hearing of him, and I also remember what a lively time we gave them at Bull Run. I tell you the Yankees were pretty well played out that time," and the Colonel rubbed his knees and chuckled to himself over the pleasant recollection.

"So she's Andrew Brown's widow? Well, well, I must come up and call on her before I leave town."

We all smiled, devoutly wishing that he would persuade our neighbor and her six incumbrances to remove to Green River country, Kentucky, for as Mrs. Brown had spent many years of her life in listening to the stories of Federal bravery, it would be no more than right that in her declining days she should hear the other side, and if she should eventually be urged to do so and remove from the flat, we would forever after bless our Friday evenings.

CHAPTER IV.

IN THE FIRELIGHT.

HE little red lamp shed a soft, rosy light over the room, and the fire blazed cheerily, with now and then an extra bright flame for imagination's sake. The tall lamp beside the piano had been blown out, and books and papers were strewn around, while in a corner was a suspicious-looking stand, half draped in a damp gray cloth. Now, as the firelight fell upon it, it was a beautiful woman; again a strong man in repose, and again, some fairy child.

The flat was quiet; evidently no one at home but the girl in a luxurious gown seated before the fire. Her feet, cased in red Turkish slippers, were elevated to the top of the brass fender; her head was thrown back and from it had slipped a red fez which lay on the floor; her eyes were closed, and around the deep corners of her mouth and slightly parted lips there played a smile—or was it the firelight ? Regularly the breaths came, and deep; the maiden slept. A little Dutch clock on the mantel pointed the hour of ten.

The other girls had gone to the opera, and after a hard day's work at her studio, the Duke had come home, dined alone, and donning gown and slippers had begun a little sketch for the Woman's Building.

The ideas formed themselves too slowly for her quick perception of form, and, throwing aside her tools, she had put out the largest lamp and seated herself to "study it out." And the ideas, like the flames in front of her, blazed

49

and died away until her tired and overworked mind refused to answer, and sleep, the heaven of the intellect,
dawned upon her. Over her chair leaned a handsome, dark
head; two eyes, whose depths few saw, looked upon her,
and round her waist stole an arm and strong white hand;
the other grasped hers as it lay on her knee, and the light

" MARJORIE, SEATED IN THE HAMMOCK, WAS DRAWING OFF A GLOVE."

revealed the prominent blue veins and slender nails of the
honest, masculine hand.

The Duke started, and as she did so her forehead touched
his lips, as he knelt beside her. For an instant a fearful
look came in her eyes, but as she gazed into his, all fear
departed, and deep, trustful love beamed forth; and, with

a sigh of relief, abandon-
ment and rest, she laid
her head upon his
shoulder.

"Are you ready, dear-
est, will you come with
me?"

A deep, baritone voice
spoke, like the full stop
of an organ, whose power
and gentleness carries all
before it.

"Come with you?
Why, and where?"

" Come, because I have
waited so long for your
coming; come to me and
rest. Complete my life;
give me love; all else I
have."

Did he know to whom
he spoke? Was it to the
proud, imperious, inde-
pendent Duke he talked
of filling another's life?
He *did* know, for her ideal
knelt beside her; a man
to honor, love, work for,
die for, live for.

Where had he come
from? Who was he? It
mattered not; two souls

had met, she knew what he was, and her head and heart, worn out in their struggle to conquer the world alone, lay quiet on his breast.

"Why came you so late, dear?"

"'The time is only now ripe, sweetheart; you must have suffered and worked and learned all you know alone to be willing to come with me;" and now, with a quick, impulsive gesture, he took her in his arms; and she, like a true woman, clung to the strength and good that was in him.

A peal of laughter, a stumble at the door, a knob quickly turned, and in came the girls and their escorts. She rose, desolate, forsaken, her arms out before her, a lonely feeling and a chill in her heart. Was it the laugh of a demon? Had her love disappeared like a phantom?

"Hello, Duke! asleep, old girl?" Marjorie, seated in the hammock, began drawing off a glove; Gene, in her opera-cloak, stood before her, and then she knew it was a dream. The fancy of an over-worked woman's brain that needed rest and love.

CHAPTER V.

(To which the fiat owes its being.)

WHEN the World's Fair Bill was under discussion by the Fifty-first Congress, Mr. Wm. T. Springer, of Illinois, rose one bright morning with an amendment.

The general bill had provided for the formation of a Commission, and the amendment added that " said Commission is authorized and required to appoint a Board of Lady Managers, of such number and to perform such duties as may be prescribed by the Commission." When the bill was reported to the house for a final hearing, the amendment was not read. Mr. Springer called attention to the omission, and the chairman of the committee replied that it was unintentional—the amendment having been left out because the committee considered it of no importance whatever, but that if desired it could yet be restored to the bill, and this was consequently done.

Mr. Springer offered his amendment as a graceful tribute to the women of our country, and it was passed by Congress without a dissenting voice, and without one thought of the importance of the measure which was to give legal right, for the first time in the history of any nation, to the organization of a body of women to transact business for the Government.

The women themselves, who were appointed under this act in the various States, did not realize for one moment the responsibility and power thus given them, and when for the first time the Board of Lady Managers was convened in Chicago in November, 1890, there was much hesitation and a great lack of knowledge as to the object of its existence and the future possibilities which lay before it.

It was a representative body of women that gathered in the pretty hall at Kinsley's that bright, crisp, November morning. Some had had experience with parliamentary law in their charitable and club work at home, but the majority were totally untutored in business methods and came together with a feeling of hesitation that prevented them from giving utterance to their ideas. Some were business women, school teachers, farmers, lawyers and physicians, while one woman was most successful as a real estate dealer, and another had charge of a valuable plantation in Louisiana. Several owned or edited newspapers, but by far the greater number were the wives and mothers who had come, for the first time, to take part in public affairs. On every hand the question was asked, "What are we here for?" and no one seemed to answer. The Commissioners, when appealed to, were as much at sea as their appointees on the Board of Lady Managers, but all agreed that the first thing to do was to effect a permanent organization. In accordance with this, committees were formed, by-laws made, and Mrs. Potter Palmer, of Chicago, was elected President.

When the meeting adjourned, the ladies had become somewhat acquainted with each other and had voted upon several questions of importance, especially upon having no separate exhibit of women's work at the Exposition. It was conceded by all that competitors would wish to receive awards upon the basis of merit and not of sex, and that in consequence the best exhibitors would not send their work

unless for general competition. It was also agreed that it would be a good plan to ask the Directors of the World's Fair for a building in which a special exhibit could be shown that would demonstrate to the world the progress that women had made in the nineteenth century.

When the members left the city, all these undeveloped suggestions were left in the hands of the President, a young woman who had had no experience whatever in public affairs. It has been widely recorded how well she performed her task, and when the Board met for the second time, in September, '91, it was on an entirely different plane, and with the brightest prospects of future usefulness. The first circular sent out from the office of the Board asked the members to petition their legislatures to secure an appropriation for the World's Fair, and to request at the same time that the members of the Board of Lady Managers be recognized on the State Board. In many States this was done, giving these women an entirely unprecedented authority, and to their credit be it said, that in many instances the legislators acknowledged that their attention had first been brought to the World's Fair through the efforts of these women.

The Board asked the officers in charge of the Installation Department to place on the blanks they were sending out to manufacturers the innocent little question, "Do you employ any women in the manufacture of this article, and if so, what proportion of it is their work?" There have been many responses, and as every article manufactured in whole or in part by women is to bear some graceful device showing the fact, it will be readily seen that to those interested, the World's Fair will present the most remarkable display of women's work that has ever been made public, and the heretofore unrepresented factory woman will receive her due share of credit for the work she has done.

Congress in its original action had decided that the

Board of Lady Managers might be allowed to have one or more members on the juries which were to award prizes for articles which had been in whole or in part manufactured by women. This gave a power to the Board which was entirely unprecedented, for no women have ever been allowed to serve as jurors in previous expositions.

When the subject came up for consideration at a later time, the Commission agreed to this without the slightest hesitation, and so little conception did the members have of the extent of this work, that they offered at first to allow the juries to be composed entirely of women that were to judge of women's work.

When it was afterwards discovered that women are employed in nearly every branch of industry, this gracious permission was modified to allowing women members on the juries in proportion to the amount of women's work represented in the articles to be judged. Even this was an enormous concession, as the recently appointed Committee on Juries is just beginning to realize.

No one could question the fairness of allowing women as jurors *in proportion to the amount of women's work represented in the article to be judged,* and yet when one takes into consideration the fact that women have not heretofore been allowed this privilege, and also that it would be yielding up much power and political patronage to allow women the appointing of a number of jurors, it seems that the action of the Commission in this regard was not only fair and honorable, but noble and high-minded.

It is to be hoped that the Commission which has from the first treated the Board of Lady Managers with great courtesy and absolute fairness, will never by any future action change this ruling which has won it the praise and gratitude of every thinking woman in the nation.

In January, 1891, when the subject of a National appropriation for the year for the World's Fair was under discussion, and enemies of the bill were very anxious to have a small amount named, the President of the Board of Lady Managers and the Finance Committee went to Washington to see what might be done. When they arrived they found matters in the most unpromising state. The bill had in the Senate been cut down to $40,000, which was not enough for the running expenses of the Commission alone, and no allowance had been made for the wants of the Board of Lady Managers. The Finance Committee and the President had an interview with the Senate Committee to which this matter had been referred, which had a direct and acknowledged result of raising the amount from $40,000 to $95,500, of which sum $36,000 was named for the exclusive use of the Board of Lady Managers. This was a great triumph and occasioned much rejoicing among the members of the Board, who had felt that a failure to secure an appropriation would make them entirely dependent on the Commission, would certainly restrict their future usefulness, and might imperil their very existence. One of the principal arguments used in presenting the case to the Senators was the fact that the Directors of the World's Fair had graciously given to the Board the sum of two hundred thousand dollars with which to erect a building for the exclusive use of women, which should be known as the Woman's Building.

The Board of Lady Managers met for the second time in Apollo Hall, and it was no longer a gathering of strangers, trying to find a familiar face, or identify some well-known name with some strange personality. It was more like a meeting of friends, and there was laughter and general cheer, for the Board had had its trials as well as its victo-

ries, which had bound more closely together the members
from the various states. The ladies all knew each other,
at least by correspondence, and many were the rejoicings
at this meeting. The President's desk was a mass of lilies
and roses and fragrant sweet peas, and the young President
herself, in light gray gown, returned the many greetings
with smiling face, while at her left presided the able secre-

THE FAVORITE USHER.

tary, Mrs. Cooke. Three or four pretty children acted as
pages, while Mrs. Logan's niece—a charming young girl—
was decidedly the favorite usher.

At the November meeting, the prominent members had
been those whose reputation and experience gave them the
right to be heard, and while their influence was no less
strong at the second meeting, yet many new voices had
gained confidence to speak, though one of the most elo-

quent and beloved—Mrs. Darby's, of South Carolina—was missing.

Among the ladies present who had achieved national reputation were Mrs. Logan and Mrs. Hooker. Mrs. Logan was a tall, commanding-looking woman, whose gray hair, brushed straight back from her intellectual forehead, gave her an air of distinction. She wore deep mourning, and when she spoke talked straight to the point, while her tact and diplomacy showed her knowledge and long association with politicians. Mrs. Hooker was another striking and interesting character, and her piquant remarks added much to the zest of the meeting. She was of medium height, with marked features, clear complexion, beautiful snowy curls and a peculiar, petulant toss of the head that is a characteristic of the Beecher family, I am told. Mrs. Barker, of South Dakota, with her strong face and clear logic won the most complete attention, while Mrs. Meredith, of Indiana, was convincing in debate; but Mrs. Eagle, of Arkansas, was the best parliamentarian on the Board, and brought the ladies to strict account if by any chance they spoke twice to the same subject.

There was Mrs. Russell Harrison, with her pretty face and sweet manners, and her charming friend, Mrs. Salisbury, of Utah, who is the favorite niece of Mr. James G. Blaine. There were also the wives of the Governors of Montana and Maine, Arkansas, Mississippi and other States. There were a score of others, too, who made most interesting speeches. Mrs. Lucas, of Philadelphia; Mrs. Ashley, of Colorado; Mrs. Reed, of Maryland; Mrs. Lynde and Ginty, of Wisconsin; Mrs. Bagley, of Michigan; Miss Beck, of Florida; Miss Shakespeare, of Louisiana; Mrs. Houghton, of Washington; Mrs. Oglesby and Mrs. Shepard, of

"THE SWELL MEMBER."

Illinois; Mrs. Starkweather, of Rhode Island; Mrs. Bradwell and Mrs. Mulligan, of Chicago; Mrs. Wilkins, of Washington; Mrs. Cantrill, of Kentucky; Mrs. Ryan, of Texas, Miss Busselle, of New Jersey; Mrs. Felton, of Georgia; Mrs. Trautman, of New York, and others, while Mrs. Payton, of Oregon, whose voice before had been unheard, convulsed the large audience many times with her witty remarks.

I have said nothing of the appearance of these women, but their faces were all bright and intelligent, while, for the lovers of society, there were many pretty women, from the graceful member from western Illinois, to the swell little member from New York, whose light-trained dress, with its high, black sleeves, was an object of general admiration to the rows of spectators who filled every available inch in the parlors behind the President's desk.

Many prominent and well-known gentlemen attended these meetings, and among them on several occasions was seen the strong face of Prof. Swing, whom I heard several lady managers point out to each other as Mrs. Palmer's husband.

There could be nothing more attractive than the manner in which the President presided over the meeting. Her ease and grace, and the winning way in which she recognized each member who took the floor, were altogether charming, while her parliamentary knowledge was a complete surprise. The deliberations, while full of interest to all, were marked by a dignity and ease that were most impressive.

Before the second meeting of the full Board, a letter had been prepared, which was signed by the President of the Board of Lady Managers, and sent officially, through the courtesy of Mr. Blaine and the Department of State, to every country in the world. It asked that the government of the country addressed should appoint a commission of women to coöperate with the Board of Lady Managers in preparing an exhibit from their country that should show the finest and best work that women have done from the earliest known times to the present day. This request was sent not only in the hope of securing a fine exhibit of women's work from each foreign country, but with the special intention of obtaining recognition for women by their own government. This was particularly to be desired in the countries where women had not been recognized as fully as in the United States.

It is not necessary to give the details of the State correspondence, but it is enough to say that the result thus far has exceeded all expectations. In nearly every instance the sovereign of the country addressed has sent a courteous reply to the President of the Board of Lady Managers, and in many instances Commissions have already been formed and are in working order.

In England the Woman's Commission, which is doing splendid work, is under the immediate patronage of the Princess Christian, who is a member of the Royal family. In Germany, the Princess Friedrich Karl has given the formation of the sub-committees her personal attention. The Queen of Belgium has graciously consented to appoint a commission of women in her dominion; while in Russia, Sweden, Holland, Greece, Austria, and France the commissions have either been formed or are in process of organization, and in all cases under the highest patronage. Letters have also been received from Japan and the Orient in regard to the subject, while such distant rulers as the Queen of Hawaii, the Governor-General of Cape Town, of

Jamaica, and of Cuba and Hayti, in the West Indies, have expressed their willingness to appoint these Commissions. The women of Central and South America are also actively

engaged in collecting their exhib- its, and Madame Diaz, the honored wife of the President of Mexico, has written expressing her cordial approval and in- terest in the plans of the Board of Lady Managers.

The Woman's Building, which I have incidentally men- tioned, was planned by a young girl, aged twenty-one, whose designs were successful in the competition offered by the Board of Lady Managers. Miss Hayden is of medium height, slender, with soft, dark hair, and a pleasant manner that is shy, without the least lack of confidence. She is a graduate of the Four Years' Course of the Boston Institute of Technology, where she was one of the most brilliant and earnest pupils. She is of Spanish parentage, and inherits the soft, dark eyes of the Latin race; though, perhaps, it is her long residence in Boston that has made her so quiet and reserved. She is always willing to talk of her work, but says that she has been obliged to devote so much time to study that she has been unable to acquire the arts that make society attractive. She won the highest praise from the architects with whom she was associated in making the working drawings of the Woman's Building. Mr. Burnham expressed himself as very much pleased with her and said that she had great adaptability, and could readily seize a new idea, while it was generally known about the Construction Department that no one could change, by any amount of persuasion, one of her plans when she was convinced of its beauty or originality. She was always quiet but generally carried her point.

The building that she has planned is two hundred by four hundred feet, and in the severe but elegant style of the Italian renaissance. It went up with marvelous rapidity, and was finished far in advance of any other structure on the grounds. The frame-work is covered with staff, a kind of composition, which hardens to almost the consistency of granite, and which readily receives any beautiful tint. It has been colored a rich old ivory, to harmonize with the prevailing tone of the surrounding structures. A series of open colonnades, supporting balconies, surrounds the building, and from the stone-carved balustrades depend trailing

vines from baskets of flowers placed at short intervals. Above the second story, great stone caryatides support the roof garden.

HE clay models for these figures were designed and molded by Miss Enid Yandell, of Louisville, Kentucky, who at the early age of twenty-two has much reputation as a sculptor. This roof garden is one of the most charming places imaginable, with its high, arching palms, and the various ferns and flora that have been contributed through members of the Board of Lady Managers all over the country. The pediment over the wide entrance and the beautiful groups on the cornices of the building are the work of Miss Alice Rideout, of San Francisco, who received the prize in the competition. She is a very attractive young girl, only nineteen years of age, with blonde hair and a sweet, open face.

Of the interior of the building I shall say but little, as it is too large a subject, but its high-arched, central hall, called the Gallery of Honor, with its beautiful works of art, all executed by women; its library, its model hospital and sanitary kitchen will all combine to make it a source of comfort to every woman visiting the Exposition, as it will undoubtedly be a pride and joy to the members of the Board that created it.

It has been suggested that the Sunday-school children all over the country donate banners to the Woman's Building. These could bear the name of the class, and be of all shapes and colors; and it would be delightful to name a day which should be called Children's Day, when all the little folks could come in a procession and plant their banners around the balcony in the Gallery of Honor, where they would float as proudly as those of the Knights of the Bath in Westminister Abbey, or the signals of Napoleon's triumphs in the Hôtel des Invalides, at Paris.

Many offers have already been made for the decoration of the Woman's Building, Mrs. Houghton, of Washington, being the pioneer in this direction, by the presentation of a beautiful pair of marble columns from the women of her State. Since then the various members have offered the products of their States and Territories in the form of carved light wood panels for the drawing-rooms, balustrades for the grand staircases, hammered brass, slabs of onyx and black marble, tapestries and hangings, granite steps, and last, but not least, the famous nail of copper, silver and

GROUP ON WOMANS' BUILDING.

gold from Montana, which is to complete the building, and to be driven by the President of the Board. Nebraska has volunteered to send the hammer to drive the nail. Idaho, the block into which it is to be driven, and Colorado, the jewel-case which is to contain it, and which is to be an act copy in miniature of the mineral palace of Pueblo.

Fretwork reading-desks, rich windows of stained glass, Navajo blankets for portières, petrified wood panels, cactus-wood screens, and numberless other articles have been offered from various sources.

Florida has promised a standard for electricity, to be made of polished pink marble.   It is to represent a palmetto

CHILDREN'S DAY.

tree, with the lights shining through t h e tufted leaves that crown the smooth trunk, and was designed by a young girl of eighteen years.

A wrought-iron drinking-fountain has b e e n offered b y Northern Michigan, and the women of Buena Vista, Colorado,have also volunteered to furnish one for the roof-garden.   The design for this fountain is very unique and represents a beautiful peak overlooking the smiling valley of Buena Vista.   Down the slope of the hill a bear is seen approaching a spring where a flood of crystal water gushes forth into a pool and forms the basin of the fountain. The figures of this remarkable design are to be carved from solid red sandstone. The women of Denver have planned to place a beautiful pavilion in the Woman's Building, which shall display women cutting, polishing and setting gems, and will give the public a glimpse of an entirely new industry.

One member has suggested, that she may send an exact copy of the beautiful piece of needle-work on which Mary Queen of Scots was engaged at the time of her execution, the needle sticking just as it was left by the ill-fated queen, and many other historic relics have been promised.

The women of California were the first to ask to furnish an entire room in the Woman's Building, and their plans have already assumed definite shape. The floor and ceiling of this large apartment are to be of laurel, inlaid with the various woods from California, while the walls are all solid redwood, relieved by occasional panels of canvas painted by the best women artists in the State. The subject for the mural decorations will be the cactus, which will be used in every possible way. Wreaths of this blossom, as delicate and varied as the orchid, are to be ground in the natural colors into the opalescent glass of the windows. All the hangings and draperies will be in the cactus colorings, the groundwork being the dull, gray green of the foliage, which contrasts beautifully with the shaded tints of the blossoms. Great vases of this plant, in full bloom, will be scattered throughout the room. The women of New York will probably decorate and furnish the library, and this will be done under the supervision of Mrs. Candace Wheeler, whose beautiful tapestries and art fabrics are so well known. The women of West Virginia have also undertaken to furnish and decorate a room, and the women of Kansas City have made the same offer.

The women of Cincinnati will furnish and decorate two rooms, and when one remembers the artistic reputation that city bears, with its beautiful glazed Rookwood pottery, its noted wood carvings, its terra cottas and its paintings, wonderful results are expected.

The exhibit in the Woman's Building is not supposed to be of a general character, for it must not be forgotten that the work that women have done is scattered through all the buildings according to the classification, being entered in the various competitions with that of men. The exhibit in the Woman's Building is simply an object lesson of the very finest work done by the women of all countries, and designed to show the progress they have made since liberty and education have been granted them. Hundreds of applications have been received for space in the Woman's Building. Queen Margherita, of Italy, has offered her priceless collection of laces, and there will also be a display from Russia, Austria, Ireland, and even far-away Africa, of exquisite embroideries and laces.

Lady Aberdeen has asked for space, and wishes to display the wax figures of a bride and all her maids clothed in exquisite Irish point lace. A complete household equipment of Irish linen will also be shown. Messrs. Marshall Field & Co. have already bought the bride's dress and will exhibit it after the Exposition has closed. Hayward's, the best known lace-house in London, has asked to show a historical collection of rare old laces, and the Princess Narischkine desires to send from Russia an exhibit of the laces and the silver embroidered costumes made by the peasants on her vast estate. But it is quite impossible to enumerate the many interesting objects that have been offered in various lines.

The Board of Lady Managers wished to emphasize particularly the progress of women in a business and professional way, and in this connection will show the finest work they have done in the various lines, such as illustrating, wood-engraving, painting, sculpture, wood-carving, designing for wall paper, carpets, fabrics, etc., as well as a complete showing of journalistic and literary work.

The Board also intends to make a fine archæological exhibit which will show woman as the inventor of the industrial arts and the first maker of the home. The officers in charge of the Smithsonian Institute at Washington have kindly volunteered to lend to the Woman's Building such objects as may be desired, and this valuable collection will be supplemented by others taken from museums and private collections both in this country and Europe. The recent discoveries in New Mexico and Arizona will be represented in this display, and considerable space will be given to the valuable collection recently made by Mrs. French-Sheldon, who followed Stanley's footsteps far into the interior of Africa. Mrs. French-Sheldon proposes to exhibit not only her curios, but the caravan in which she traveled. It may be remembered that she was the first woman to penetrate the interior of Africa, and that she always received the chiefs in a white silk ball gown with long train instead of rough traveling costume, and they bowed down to her like a queen and yielded up their choicest treasures; while the women and children, instead of running away in fright, came for miles to touch her hand.

Many applications have been received from prominent associations of women physicians and dentists, as well as numerous organizations of all kinds. The library will contain the best books written by the women of all countries;

and, if possible, the manuscripts of famous books with the original illustrations will be displayed. Authentic pictures of women renowned in history and literature will be furnished by the foreign committees to adorn this room.

The plans of the Board of Lady Managers have so widened since the first meeting at Kinsley's and so many new vistas have opened, that it is impossible here to describe the work in detail or predict where it will end. The Dormitory Association has planned to establish four dormitories which will take care of five thousand industrial women each night at a maximum cost to the individual of forty cents. This work is under the immediate supervision of Mrs. Matilda B. Carse, who superintended the great W. C. T. U. Temple at Chicago, and who is a member of the Board. The secretary is Mrs. Helen M. Barker, who has also undertaken the preparation of an encyclopædia of women's organizations which shall represent every branch of organized work in which women have engaged.

A delightful plan has been projected for a Children's Palace, which is to provide a safe place where children can be left while their mothers visit the various departments of the Exposition. The building, which is to be a dainty and beautiful blue and white structure, will contain everything which can conduce to the comfort and pleasure of childhood, including lecture-rooms and kindergartens for the older children, nurseries with sanitary food and trained attendants for the babies, and toys for all.

The flat roof, with its high stone balustrade, covered at a height of fifteen feet, with a strong wire netting, will form an ideal play-ground. Within this charming enclosure, which will be bordered by vines and flowers, birds and butterflies will flit among the children at will, the wire covering rende-ing cages unnecessary. An awning will protect from sun and rain. Mrs. George L. Dunlap is chairman of the committee in charge of this work, and has been doing valiant service in raising the necessary funds, for the Children's Building and the Dormitory have both been paid for outside of the appropriation given to the Board.

Any child or club of children sending one dollar to the Children's Home will receive a printed certificate of acknowledgment, bearing the official seal of the Board of Lady Managers.

All these buildings will be monuments to the progress women have made during the nineteenth century, but I feel that the greatest object accomplished by the Board of Lady Managers will be the showing of the work done by the industrial women in this and all other countries. The object lesson it will teach to the nations of the world cannot soon be forgotten, and perhaps these long silent sisters will at last have an opportunity for the pay and the freedom that should be accorded them as equal laborers in the world's great workshop.

CHAPTER VI.

MR. PERKINS.

THE morning was bright and sunny. Gene had been to church and had walked on the Lake-Shore Drive afterward with Mr. Middleton, who came in with her when they reached the flat. She had brought home the little printed circular containing the morning's hymns, and on entering sat down at the piano, without removing her wraps, and commenced, softly, to play them over. Mr. Middleton stood looking down at her—we all think he is very fond of Gene—and how was it that the music drifted to the nightingale's song, and that Gene, who is always so good, forgot that it was Sunday and commenced to sing, in her sweet voice, "Ah, no, I cannot forget you?" Suddenly, she became conscious of a foreign presence in the room, and turned her head, when, to her surprise, her glance fell upon a stranger. It was rather an embarrassing moment, and as she rose with a flush on her face, the stranger stepped toward them and said, inquiringly, "Mr. Perkins?" Gene answered at once, "I fear you have made a mistake, which is a very common thing

with so many apartments in one building. Mr. Perkins
does not live here." "Oh no," the young man answered,
with perfect self-possession, "*I* am Mr. Perkins, and I have
come to see Miss Wendell." "Oh, I beg your pardon,"
cried Gene, blushing. "She is not in the city. She went
to spend Sunday in Evanston." "I know it," replied the

young man, "but I have an appointment to meet her at a
quarter after one, as I am going with her to dinner at her
cousin, Mrs. Dickey's." It was then almost the moment
mentioned, so he sat down to wait, while Marjorie came in
from Sunday School and joined them.

Mr. Perkins proved to be a very amusing and interesting
young man, with light, curly hair, a frank, open face, and a
manner that was at once deferential and yet showed a desire to please. He told them that he had lived in Wash-

ington, and gave them many stories of Western life, so
that the time slipped by with great rapidity, and Katie had
announced the two-o'clock dinner, before anyone noticed
that the Duke had not arrived. "Won't you come to
dinner with us?" asked Virginia. "There is surely some
mistake, and as you are a stranger in Chicago it would
be very awkward for you to dine alone, down town, at a
hotel." He hesitated a moment, and then said: "I wonder if you would ever forgive me if I did do such an un-
conventional thing? The truth is that I should like immensely to stay." And so the matter was settled without
more ado.

They were at dinner when a ring came at the door, and
Katie said that someone wished to speak to Miss Fairfax.
Gene left the room and returned in a moment, dimpling
with laughter, to say that it was a young man whom
she had never before met, who asked for her, as he was so
much surprised to find that Miss Wendell was not in, as he
had an engagement to go to dinner with her at her cousin,
Mrs. Dickey's. Mr. Perkins was very much amused and
the dinner progressed with great jollity, as he and Mr.
Middleton, who found that they belonged to the same Col-
lege fraternity, vied with each other in telling stories and
anecdotes.

The dessert was on the table, when Katie was called
away by another ring at the door, and returned in a
few moments with her good Irish face settled into a grin
that stretched from ear to ear, as she said that it was some
young gentleman who wouldn't leave his name, but who
seemed very much surprised to learn that Miss Wendell was
not in, as he had an engagement to go with her to dinner
at her cousin, Mrs. Dickey's.

At this we all shouted, until the old maid who always sits in the bathroom in the top flat, to tell the gossip that she hears floating up through the shaft, must have had something to repay her for her long vigil.

It was seven o'clock at night when the Duke came in, a disconsolate wretch—for the face of that little hypocrite, which is the merriest in the world when she laughs, can be drawn down to such an expression of melancholy that the hardest-hearted person in the world could not help forgiving her sins. I never could remember just what explanation she made, but as it was perfectly satisfactory to Mrs. Dickey and to the young men, including Mr. Perkins, who soon called again, it does not make much difference.

CHAPTER VII.

GENE'S BURGLAR.

MUST write down my horrible experience of Friday night, now that I am able to sit up and think coherently.

It was very late when Marjorie and I started home. The car was crowded, as usual at that time in the evening, there being more men than women. We sandwiched ourselves into a small space, given us by a polite man, and I clutched my pocket in which—foolish girl that I was—I had three hundred dollars. This money had been received that day from the sale of some land, which had been for a long time in the family, and I had cashed the check in the afternoon, thinking I would pay a few bills on my way down town in the morning. I whispered to Marjorie to pay our fare, as I didn't care to take out my purse. "Oh, did you get the money, Virginia?" "Yes," I assented, under my breath. "What a lucky girl! You will surely have to treat the flat." "Be careful, Marjorie!" and as I cautioned her to speak more softly, I caught the expression of a man's face just across from us. He was a coarse-looking man and wore a slouch hat pulled down over his face. He gave Marjorie a quick, piercing look, and I saw an ugly, red-looking scar over his left eye, while his thick lips were only half-hidden under his black whiskers. Altogether he was what a man out West would call an "ugly customer." He paid no further attention to us, and in talking of other things I had forgotten him entirely until we got out of the car at Chicago avenue, when, to our dismay,

he got off too, and sauntered along leisurely behind
us with his hat very far down over his eyes. We ran all
the way down the block, and I was glad, indeed, to get into
the house.

I felt a little uncomfortable even after reaching
the warmth and light of our own little flat, and some-

"WAS THAT TALL, BLACK THING OUTLINED ON THE CURTAIN THE PIANO LAMP?"

thing impelled me to go to the window. I pulled back the
curtain and looked out, and there, under the lamp on the
opposite side of the street, stood the man looking up at me!
My feelings were anything but agreeable after that, but
the other girls reassured me—telling of the night-watchman,
of how many men there were in the same building to be
summoned at a moment's notice, etc., etc. Somewhat paci-
fied I went in to dinner, and afterwards we spent a merry
evening with a number of friends, and I forgot all about

the man. Before I retired I took the money and pinned it
into the crown of an old hat, underneath the lining, and
hung the hat up in the closet, as that was always my own
private safe-deposit vault.

Dismissing all thoughts of fear I opened the window
for some fresh air and retired. I can't tell how long I
had slept when I was suddenly awakened by a strange
noise, and all my faculties became keenly alive.
Through the folding-doors I saw the moonlight streaming
in at the parlor windows, and the curtain swaying gently
backward and forward. Was that tall, black thing outlined
on the curtain the piano lamp? I strained my eyes to
see, not daring to move. As I gazed, the black object
moved across the room, and a silent match flashed a light
upon the face of the wretched man whom we had seen
on the car. Yes, there was no use in trying to disbelieve
it; there was the slouch hat, the scar and the ugly, thick
lips. In the instant that the match flashed I saw that he
had a second man with him. They had climbed up to the
balcony and come in by the window that I had left open.
I knew that the Duke kept both the doors to her room
closed and locked, and I wished with all my heart for
the much despised pistol. Marjorie slept in the room
at the end of the hall, out of hearing, and I was alone
with those two horrible robbers who knew that I had three
hundred dollars in my possession! All these things flashed
through my mind; I grew rigid with fear. I opened my
mouth and tried to call the Duke, for I knew that she was
the nearest, but I could not make a sound. By this time the
leader of the two men had lit a bull's-eye lantern, and as
he flashed the light around the parlor, he caught sight of
my bed in the back room. " Here, Bill, don't make a noise.

This is the one that had the cash," and threw the light full
on my face, which must have been as pale as death. It
took all my strength of mind not to move an eyelid, and
the second the light rested on me seemed an eternity.
They finally turned their attention to the bureau, and began picking up the few articles of jewelry that I had left
there. The next thing they did was to rummage in the
bureau drawers, and as their backs were turned to me I felt
this was the critical moment, and now or never I must act.

Not far from the head of my bed was a large closet which
opened into Marjorie's room. The door leading into her
room from the closet was closed, I knew, but the one leading into my room had been removed and a portière hung
over the opening. If I could get into the closet without
their seeing me, I could open the door and rush into Marjorie's room, and there, at least, we two could fight together. I
climbed out of bed expecting every moment to see them
turn, as they were muttering to themselves over not finding
the money. How I managed it without making some
slight noise I never knew; but there I was on the floor, at
last, creeping along by the wall to the curtain. How far it
seemed!—and how cold I was with fear! But I knew my one
chance of escape was to get into that other room. With a
noiseless wave of the curtain I found myself in the closet,
and sent up a prayer of thankfulness. I could hear the
men opening the boxes in my bureau, and their comments
on the things they wished to take. I straightened myself
up, took one long stride to the closet door—I turned the
handle, it creaked audibly; it seemed to stick—great heav-
ens, it was locked! There was a commotion in the next
room; the lantern was flashed on my bed. "She's got out
and gone, Bill, quick, behind that curtain!" They jerked

back the curtain, the lantern flashed on me, I saw the man with the scar point his pistol at me and then I knew no more, for I fell head first against the door.

The next I knew I found myself on the bed with the two girls hanging over me, Marjorie with a pale face and the cologne bottle, while the Duke, with a determined look, was clutching her pistol with her right hand. Marjorie said she was awakened by a piercing shriek which I suppose I uttered, and a heavy fall against her closet door. When she opened the door I was lying there unconscious, and the figure of a man was just disappearing out of the front parlor window.

Sunday

CHAPTER VIII.

SUNDAY MORNING.

T was a lovely morning; the sun touched the wind-ruffled waters of the lake into myriads of flashing diamonds. The air was warm and odorous, and the rose geraniums in the window-boxes were spicy and fresh with the morning dew. The few passers-by walked slowly along the streets talking quietly to each other, filled with reverence for the Sabbath stillness. The mellow bells chimed the hour of nine in the great tower of the Cathedral on the corner, but in the little flat on Cass street all was still. Virginia was the first to wake. "Come, you lazy girls," she called, "it is after nine o'clock and Katie says that breakfast is nearly dried up with waiting." Slowly came the sounds of life from the different rooms, and soon three girls, with cheeks all pink from recent sleep, sat about the little round table in the dining-room.

"What are you going to do to-day?" asked Marjorie.

" I'm going to church, of course," said Virginia, with a sweet
look of dignity, "and you, Duke?" The great black
eyes were full of mischief as she answered, " I am going to
take a Turkish bath, and I want you girls to go with me.
Now don't look so shocked Gene, for I am really serious
about it. I'm going to listen to a sermon on the text,
'Cleanliness is next to Godliness,' and I want you to come
too. It is ridiculous for girls who have to work all the week
to try and keep up with their duties every single Sunday.
We always go to church, why shouldn't we miss just one
morning?" " But it doesn't seem respectable, does it,"
asked Marjorie, already half won over. " No, it don't *seem*
so; that is just the point, but it really is. There won't be a
soul down there, probably, and I really think it is a heap
better than staying home all day in a wrapper and reading
novels the way so many good church members do."

Here a ring at the door interrupted them, and Katie in
her clean Sunday cap entered and smilingly announced Mr.
Middleton. "Ask him in here, Katie," cried Marjorie,
while Gene's cheeks took on a deeper touch of pink, though
she made no comment. In came Mr. Middleton with three
great bunches of flowers; sweet peas for the Duke, violets
for Marjorie, and a bunch of purple pansies for Gene.
" Won't you have some breakfast ?" asked the Duke. " No,
thank you. I would like to, but I can't stay. We have
some relatives here from the East who are just returning
from a trip to Alaska, and I have promised father to take
them to church."

After he left the talk drifted to other subjects, and little
more was said about the bath, but a half hour later when
the Duke came into Marjorie's room to borrow a black pin,
she found her carefully rolling up Gene's tailor-made jacket

within her own. "What in the world are you doing," cried
the Duke. "Virginia said she wasn't going with us." "Oh,
but she will. I am sure, and I am taking her coat, as she
has a little cold. We will need our wraps even if it is such
a warm day."

The girls walked down Cass street towards the city,
when Marjorie happened to notice something in Virginia's
hand. "What have you got in that little package, Gene?"
she asked curiously. Virginia made no answer and looked
a little confused, but did not resist when the Duke took it
from her hand, and opening one end looked in. A comb
and a curling-iron met her astonished gaze, and as she
showed it to Marjorie, they both exclaimed with disgust,
"Why, you meant to go all the time."

*　　*　　*　　*　　*　　*　　*　　*　　*　　*

My Dear Will:

I must write you my usual Sunday letter, but I am really
ashamed to tell you what we have been doing to-day. In
the first place it was all that mad-cap Duke. You know
how fond we are of her, and how persuasive she is. Well,
she took it into her head to take a Turkish bath this morning, and nothing would satisfy her but to have us go with
her. It is always easy enough for me to yield, but we finally
persuaded Gene too.

State street is not a pretty or picturesque thoroughfare,
as you know, neither is it awe-inspiring; but I give you my
word I felt really ashamed of the cobble-stones and the
closed windows as we walked by this morning; especially
as we passed Central Music Hall where the late-comers
were loitering into church. When we reached the Palmer
House I think we were all willing and ready to turn back,

but of course no one would acknowledge it. The Duke walked boldly up and tried the door of the regular entrance in Madame Louise's millinery store, but found it locked, and we pretended to be glancing at the hats inside while she spoke to the colored porter at the carriage entrance, asking him if the Turkish bath was open. He was a solemn-faced

negro, with black excrescences on his face and neck, like the fungus on a tree, and when she asked him that question, he rolled up his eyes until you could see nothing but the whites, then brought them to a cross-eyed focus on the Duke's nose, while he said solemnly, in guttural tones: "No mam, they ain't no Turkish bath open on Sunday, leastwise none that I eber herd tell on," then raising his hands to heaven, big white cotton gloves and all, "Six days

shalt thou labaw, an do all thou hez to do, for in six days
the Lawd made heben, and earth, the sea and all that are
in dem, and rested on the seventh and hollowed, therefore,
chillun ye must do no manner of work, ye, nor your neigh-
baw, nor your ox, nor anything that is yourne." The Duke
laughed for two blocks, but I honestly think that we all
felt guilty at the old darkey's lecture.

We discussed what we should do
next, and the Duke was for telephon-
ing the Grand Pacific to see if we
could get in there, but we had no
place from which to send a message
except a drug store, and none of us
liked to ask that question in public.
As we walked back on State street
we found that it was growing very
warm, especially as we had to carry
our wraps, which were unnecessary
in the bright sunshine, and as we
passed Central Music Hall, Gene
said timidly: "I wonder if it is too
late to hear the sermon?" We could
hear the big organ pealing forth
within, and that decided the Duke,

who is passionately fond of music. As for me, I did not
need to consider, for you know how much I love to hear
Professor Swing's lectures.

So we went in, intending to sit quietly on the red velvet
sofa by the stairs in the back of the church, and not try to
find a seat. You remember the sofa, I know—the refuge in
thought of all the people who come in late. In thought, I
say, for one generally enters to find it occupied. So it was

with us, and as we stood there a moment undecided, a gentleman with gray hair, and a beautiful, benevolent face, came up and asked us to follow him, saying he had three seats for us. At first I tried to protest, as I was in advance; but not wishing to refuse at such a moment, we followed, to be shown into one of the most conspicuous places in the house—Mrs. Medill's box. After the rustle of our entrance we were glad to subside, and presently forgot our discomfort in the opening words of that wonderful sermon. I do not need to tell you what a feast it was, for you have heard Prof. Swing; but that awkward, and to a stranger, homely man, seems to me to be almost inspired. All that he says

appeals to the reason, the imagination and the heart. His allusions show the learning of a scholar, and yet he is never pedantic. His standpoint is that of a philosopher, and yet he is tolerant of those of us of lesser stature, who go about blinded by the glamour or the follies of our century. Gifted with magnetic power that chains, from the moment he speaks, the entire attention of his hearers, he tells us, as simply as a child, the difference between right and wrong. His creed is to raise the fallen, to help the suffering, and to teach to all men the gentleness and charity that broaden the age.

But I always enthuse on this subject. Gene, as you know, is a stranger here, and had never heard him preach; and once, when I happened to glance at her, I saw that she was intensely interested in every word that he said. Her eyes gleamed in excitement—you remember their strange lapis-lazuli tint—and a ray of sunlight gilded the little tendrils of hair about her neck and temples. I saw several people looking at her, and I do not wonder; for she is a most charming creature when that perfect calm is stirred to animation. She told me afterward that she felt as if the iron had entered her soul when she thought of the iniquity she had planned earlier in the morning. I must confess that I was not afflicted with remorse, for I am not so good as Gene by nature; but I could understand her feelings, for after one of those soul-touching sermons, the stereotyped words of the average preacher seem as flavorless as Dead Sea apples.

The iron didn't enter the Duke's soul just then, but it did a few minutes later; for she was carrying Gene's little bundle, and so far forgot herself as to rise abruptly for the benediction, thereby dropping her burden. The paper broke, of course, and in the solemn stillness the little curling-iron hied itself merrily down several steps with a loud clinkety-clank, and stopped with its handle tenderly embracing the foot of the benevolent gentleman to whose courtesy we were indebted for seats. He glared at it with a look of horror, and I really believe that he did not know what it was, or where it came from, though if he had taken the trouble to turn, I am sure he could not have doubted the tell-tale aurora that en-

carnadined the face under a certain jonquil-trimmed hat.
At any rate several other people looked back, among them
three ladies, with solemn surprise on their faces, and a
young man whose brown eyes opened to their widest in a
merry laugh on seeing us. Need I say that it was Mr.
Middleton?

How much time I have taken in telling you about our
morning's adventures! But it always seems as if I could

really talk to you when I commence to write, and I never
know when to stop. Do you still sail every day in the
"Trinket," as we did last summer? Since my trip abroad this
year I am more than ever impressed with the loveliness of
our own "North Countree." Mullet Lake, in its way, is just
as beautiful as Lake Como: the same dreamy blue atmos-
phere, the same wonderfully-reflected sunsets; only Topin-
abée has a beauty of its own, a wildness and magnificence
of forest growth that we do not appreciate in the least, but
which would be enthusiastically admired by the foreigners

could they see it. How I wish I could be there for just one week! I can see you now as you started out in the morning, dressed in your corduroys and with bag and gun over your shoulder. Would you still be glad, I wonder, to take a companion who frightened away the game by talking and laughing? And would you still lay down your gun to pluck a cluster of the sweet white violets if we happened to find them?

Most sincerely,

MARJORIE.

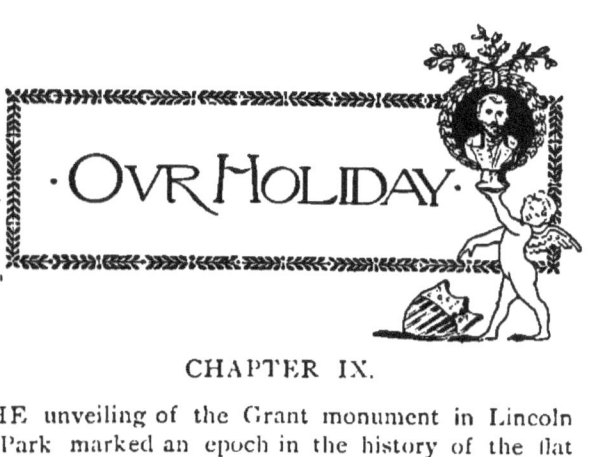

·OVR HOLIDAY·

CHAPTER IX.

THE unveiling of the Grant monument in Lincoln Park marked an epoch in the history of the flat as well as in that of Chicago, for we had a holiday, and moreover had received an invitation to go to Mrs. Palmer's in the afternoon to watch the procession from her balcony, and we were all in a consequent high state of satisfaction.

We had finished our early luncheon and commenced to dress, when a great noise of opening and shutting of drawers was heard in the Duke's room, and presently that young woman stalked forth calling in stentorian tones, "Who has seen my red gown?" Eliciting no reply she tried each room and closet but without success. Now the red gown was one of the ornaments of the flat, for it was a real, genuine, expensive, tailor-made garment of a rich shade of crimson, with a white vest heavily braided in silver. It also had a coat to match, with large buttons and high, rolling collar. And then there was a beautiful French hat, wide-brimmed, lined with crimson velvet and surmounted by masses of plumes.

Now the Duke does not usually affect Paris millinery, for she cares not a whit for dress, and is generally to be found in skirt and coat and soft felt hat, but in this attire she was always irresistible; the wide hat with its plumes

surmounting her black coils, giving, as Marjorie said, a
Lord Fauntleroy effect, so we felt naturally anxious. We
joined in the search, and calling Katie ransacked the entire flat, but to no avail. The missing garment could not
be produced.

We had wasted a half-hour, and had quite given up the
search when the Duke marched back to her room in disgust.
As she brushed by a table, her dress caught in the clay
model of a group which she had recently made, and I
noticed a grim smile of satisfaction on her face as the head
of old Father Abraham (who had been her special pride)
flew far across the room. Marjorie rushed to pick him up,
but the Duke, never uttering a word, crossed to her wardrobe and pulled out, with the air of a martyr, her old blue
dress.

It was growing late, so we hastened to our rooms once
more, when a familiar rap came at the door and we heard
Mrs. Brown's voice, saying: "What, Miss Wendell, you
home at this time of day? Now I am caught, for I just
slipped in this morning and borrowed your tailor-made
gown to copy for Ariadne, and I never meant that you
should know I had it until you saw that dear child looking
like your counterpart, for I borrowed your hat and coat
last week and copied them exactly."

I do not think it would be wise to mention in polite
society the remarks we heard in the Duke's room after
Mrs. Brown had departed.

In a few minutes we were ready and hurrying with
throngs of other people up the Lake-Shore Drive. The
houses were gay with flags and bunting, and popcorn and
peanut stands lined the street, so the scene was an animated one at every point. As we turned a corner in the

drive which brought us in view of Mrs. Palmer's house, we all uttered an exclamation of delight, for the irregular roof line, with its battlemented turrets, outlined against the blue sky, gave the appearance of an old feudal castle. A great silken flag shook out its folds in the breeze that came from the lake, and over the porte-cochère a gaily striped awning had been placed, making a pavilion from which the procession could be watched. As we entered the large

double glass door, Mrs Palmer came toward us, welcoming her guests in the high, vaulted hall. Marjorie and I saw friends in the library and went to meet them, leaving the Duke alone for a moment. What followed can best be told in her own language, as she related the incident to us that night at the dinner-table.

"I was crossing the hall when Mrs. Palmer, taking my hand, said: 'I want to introduce you to Mrs. Grant,' and as she turned toward us, 'let me present to you Miss Wendell, the young sculptor ; she is at work on the Woman's Building and we are very proud of her and think we have conferred on her an honor.' 'A sculptor! You cut marble?' I assented. 'I met one before,' she said, describing Vinnie Ream. 'She was a great deal about the General, but I don't approve of women sculptors as a rule.' Just then we were separated and I departed for the balcony to see the parade. A few minutes later, as I pushed back the black satin curtain, with its heavy gold dragons, and entered the Japanese room, I saw Mrs. Grant for an instant alone, during which I seated myself on the window ledge and took up the cudgels on behalf of working women. 'So you do not approve of me, Mrs. Grant?' 'I don't disapprove of *you*, Miss Wendell,' she replied gently, 'but I think every woman is better off at home taking care of husband and children. The battle with the world hardens a woman and makes her unwomanly.' 'And if one has no husband?' I asked. 'Get one,' she answered laconically. 'But if every woman were to choose a husband the men would not go round; there are more women than men in the world.' 'Then let them take care of brothers and fathers,' she returned. 'I don't approve of these women who play on the piano and let the children roll about on the floor, or who paint and write and embroider in a soiled gown and are all cross and tired when the men come home and don't attend to the house or table. Can you make any better housewife for your cutting marble?' 'Yes,' I answered, 'I am developing muscle to beat biscuit when I keep house.'

"'But, Mrs. Grant, are there no circumstances under which a woman may go to work?' 'I may be old-fash-

ioned; I don't like this modern movement,' she said, 'but
I don't think so; and yet, there are certain sorts of work
a woman may well do; teaching, being governess, or any
taking care of children.' 'But,' I replied, 'suppose a
case: A young brother and two strong sisters; the young
man makes a good salary but can't get ahead because all
his earnings are consumed in taking care of the girls.
Hadn't they better go to work and give him a chance to
get ahead and have a house of his own, they being as able
to work as he? Are they being unwomanly in so doing?
Or, the case of the father with a large family of girls and a
small income—are they less gentlewomen for helping earn
a living, lessening the providing of food for care of so
many mouths by adding to the family funds?'

"For a moment Mrs. Grant thought, and then, looking
far over my head, across the shining summer sea, answered:
'You may be right; in that case,' slowly, 'they ought to
go into the world.'"

After the Duke had finished talking with Mrs. Grant we
all went out on the balcony to watch the great procession
as it passed.

The throng was wonderful and I heard a gentleman say
that he had seen the crowds on Derby Day, and had been
a part of the vast concourse of people who witnessed the
Wimbledon Review in London, but never in all his life had
he seen as many people gathered together at any one time.
From the porte-cochère where Mrs. Grant reviewed the procession, the scene was superb. I have never beheld such
a mass of people. They surged over to the sea-wall on
the shore of the lake, and were packed in like sardines up
to the very doors of the house, even trampling upon the
flower-beds, as the police were powerless to resist them.

Mrs. Grant is a very warm-hearted and kindly woman, and spoke with feeling of the wonderful demonstration in honor of our hero. It was very interesting to meet so many people who have achieved prominence. General Miles, the great Indian fighter, and his interesting wife ; Mrs. Strong, widow of the late Gen. Strong ; Judge Gresham, Gen. Chetlain, young Mr. Logan, the son of Gen. Logan, besides many members of the Board of Lady Managers. The ladies all carried flowers, and waved to the orderly ranks of troops who marched by the house with uplifted hats in honor of the distinguished widow.

The bright uniforms, gay flags and stirring music were most inspiring. As the fourth division of the procession passed the house, Mrs. Grant and her son and Mr. and Mrs. Palmer took their places in the procession, and in carriages just back of them came Mrs. Palmer's guests. The ride to the grand stand was one that cannot easily be forgotten. The princely homes upon the Lake-Shore Drive were draped in flags, and for miles the streets were one dense mass of humanity. The trees upon each side of the drive were decorated with small boys, who hung on to the branches like monkeys.

As Mrs. Grant alighted from her carriage every hat was raised, and the eager faces of many scarred veterans gazed wistfully at the beloved wife of the soldier whose memory they were honoring. All down the broad avenue, spreading over the beautiful esplanade on to the wide beach beyond, and standing around the base of the monument were members of the Grand Army, and it is estimated that fully 500,000 people witnessed the ceremony. As far as the eye could reach the drive was thronged, and as the different companies marched up, each standard-bearer took his position upon the stone steps that formed the base of the monument.

The sun shone upon the hundreds of fluttering flags and gleaming bayonets, while slowly, very slowly, the flag parted and the majestic bronze figure of General Grant was

revealed to the thousands of eager spectators. In the hush that fell upon the multitude, I glanced at the wife, who was gazing upward with streaming eyes at the cold, still figure. It was not the hero, or the soldier, that she strained her eyes to see; but outlined against the sky was the face of the man she had loved. And it is little wonder that the hats of the veterans were solemnly raised, and there were few dry eyes in that vast throng as they witnessed her emotion.

The unveiling was followed by a great uproar, as the Navy and the Army vied with each other in a deafening salute.

We did not wait for the speeches but returned to the house, and spent an hour wandering about the various rooms, which the Duke had never before seen.

The interior of this stately home exceeds in grandeur

any expectations that could be formed of it. We wandered through the library, the ceiling of which is beautifully painted by a famous artist with scenes and characters from many well-known books. At one corner Juliet leaned coquettishly from her balcony, while opposite her Faust and Marguerite strolled about their garden The carved woodwork over the mantel, which was almost blackened with age, represented the full-length figures of beautiful women, and was taken, so Marjorie told us, from an old Flemish cathedral.

From this room we stepped into the little music-room, which is copied exactly from a Moorish palace. The opalescent hanging-lamps by night, and the pink-silk draperies by day, shed a roseate hue which almost warms into life the beautiful statues. We crossed the open, circular court, with its mosaic floor of Indian pattern and coloring, noting as we passed the lovely little Puck in marble by Harriet Hosmer, and the famous Nydia and Zenobia; and midway Marjorie bade us pause and raise our eyes, when lo, there burst upon our sight, through the graceful Moorish arches of the balcony, high above our heads, a cavalcade of brave knights on horseback, with crimson and golden banners outlined against the blue sky. The Duke could not resist an exclamation of surprise and delight on seeing this rich picture in stained glass.

We spent an hour in the Louis Quatorze drawing-room, where the roses, flung in handfuls on the snowy mosaic floor, gave a softness of effect that was simply marvelous. The ceiling was painted by Perraud in the most exquisite colorings; sleeping cherubs representing night nestled among the clouds and stars on one side, while others, bathed in the light of the rising sun, laughed opposite them.

The magnificent mantel of pure white onyx was laden with priceless jades, while wonderful vases of cameo, peach-blow, and Chinese "heavenly blue" reflected themselves in the mirrored walls. Snowy fur rugs were scattered over the floor at intervals, and at one end a Russian sleigh served as a chair. Slender tables stood about the

room, whose crystal tops revealed collections of marvelous curios. The first contained watches alone of rare
and curious workmanship ; one that I noticed was a beetle
not more than an inch in length, which raised its ruby
wings to display the hours ; others showed coins and
spun silver and queer Oriental jewelry—all these valuable
objects being safely locked into their transparent recep-
tacles. I shall not attempt to describe the dining-room,
with its mahogany wood-
work, its priceless tapestries,
its sideboards gleaming with
precious silver, and its fres-
coed walls, painted by the
skilful hand of Mr. John
Elliot, whose beautiful wife
is the daughter of Mrs.
Julia Ward Howe.

We glanced into the re-
ception-room with its rich
hangings and its delicate
carvings of dull teak wood ;
where rare paintings
gleamed from the dim background like jewels set in dark enamel.

Rousseau and Diaz, Corot, Millet, all were there, and I
noticed the gray-green of a Bastien-Lepage as we passed;
but Marjorie would not let us go up stairs, for she feared
that if the Duke once saw the magnificent collection of
paintings there we should never be able to get her home.

But the place that most fascinated me was the conser-
vatory. Tall palms met overhead and rare tropical plants
exhaled spicy odors, while long ferns and sweetest flowers

fringed the tesselated marble walks. The soft plash of the lake was heard in the distance, and in one charming corner swung an Indian hammock of white, braided palmetto, with its soft, crimson silk cushions. The only light at night radiates from the jeweled lamps overhead: but we were there in the afternoon, and it seemed a place where the sun-

shine loved to linger all day long.

When we reached home that night and gathered around the table in our own little dining-room, the flat had never seemed so small and shabby. Marjorie re-

marked that she had never noticed before that the papering on the wall and ceiling did not harmonize, while the
Duke cast a glance of withering scorn at our favorite
Bohemian glass vase, which happened to contain nothing
better at the moment than one limp, pink rose.   It was not
until we had tasted the steaming soup and delicious dinner
that Katie had provided that we were restored to our usual
happy confidence in ourselves and our surroundings, but
Marjorie remarked as she retired to her room that night,
that to apply Chas. Dudley Warner's sage remark, " there
is nothing like getting a new point of view," was not always
consistent with one's peace of mind.

CHAPTER X

TESSA.

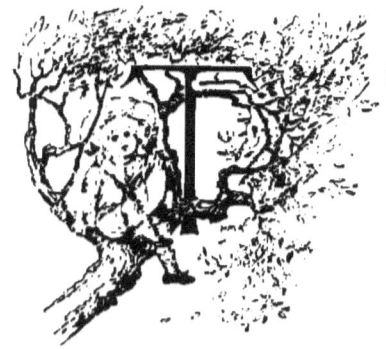

HE day had been cold and raw, with a north wind blowing, and Marjorie and the Duke had just come home and flung themselves into easy chairs, too tired to dress for dinner. The cannel fire crackled and blazed, chasing away the twilight shadows with its widening shafts of ruddy light, and the little parlor was a picture of comfort. The girls had just settled themselves when the bell rang and the peremptory rap at the door announced that the missing third had arrived.

Gene entered breathlessly, her mouth open in her eagerness to speak, her face aglow with the rush up the stairway and a soft, dark light in her eyes. "Girls!" and off went hat, coat and gloves to the floor as she talked.

"Mr. Richardson came into the office with such a sad story to-day about a young woman who had come to him for work—any work that was honest.

She was young, he said, and beautiful as a dream, though her face was worn and pallid. She seemed both proud and timid, and the supplicating manner in which she asked for employment showed that she was not accustomed to refusal, and that it hurt her to say the words that humbled her before a stranger. He said he was more touched by her manner than by her speech, for she asked him the simple question in a brief and almost forbidding way. He invited her to be seated and encouraged her to talk; and before long, emboldened, I fancy, by his kind, paternal ways and lovely old face, she told him a little of her tragic story.

After the terrible day that had wrecked her life, she had been half crazed with grief, but when her ideas returned she realized that she must make her living, and her thoughts drifted to the distant World's Fair city with its thronging strangers.

Mr. Richardson said that her narrative stopped after that, and though he tried to induce her to continue, she would say no more. Finally he asked her how long she had been in Chicago. 'Four months' she had replied. 'And you have found no work in all that time? Do you need money?' At this she broke down and confessed with great sobs that she had not touched food for two days, and that she had spent her last dollar for lodging, so that in less than a week she would be friendless and destitute in a great city. "I imagine," Gene continued, "that Mr. Richardson must have helped her, though he would not acknowledge it; but he said she would be in again the next day, when he had promised to let her know about a place. He said that he had made up this excuse to get her to return, as he did not want to lose her and she had refused to leave her address."

Marjorie was bolt upright in her chair. The Duke was on her feet and in a breath had voiced the sentiment of all, by exclaiming, "We will help her! She must come here for her meals!" Then, after thinking a moment—"My studio will afford a bed, and luckily I need a model just now and will employ her until she can get something else to do."

"But you don't know anything about her," protested Gene, feeling a sense of responsibility for the woman because she had introduced her.

Marjorie answered. "She is a woman and needs help; fate is against her, and she has come to the right place for assistance, for we have known care ourselves and will always help a woman when she is down."

That night at dinner they talked it all over, and when Gene left in the morning it was decided that she was to bring "Tessa"—for so they had named her—home with her.

*　　*　　*　　*　　*　　*　　*

It was six o'clock. Gene was late and Marjorie and the Duke stood at the window watching. Down the street came two tall, dark women; one, as they drew nearer, proved to be Gene and—the Princess! Where had she gotten her?

How proudly she carried her head! The thick veil surrounding it made it seem like a Madonna's; and what a step she had! As of a beautiful wild thing which had been caught and tamed, but was as yet unbroken.

With what an easy grace her arms swayed as she walked! Now and then she bent her head in thought or in answer to Gene.

The bell rang and the Duke opened the door.

"Tessa," said Gene (she did not know her real name), "this is our sculptor."

The woman looked up and the shadow of a smile crossed her face.

"And this is Marjorie!"

By tacit consent Christian names were used by the girls in the flat.

"We are happy to see you. We feared you might not

come ; we are so glad you did. Let me have your coat and hat."

In a moment Marjorie had taken them—and what a revelation!

A perfect, oval face; black hair which made a soft broken line around her brow, parted and coiled low on her neck, hazel eyes and a sensitive mouth with deep corners. The face was a sad one, with recent lines of care around the mouth and eyes.

Her hands were long, slender and shapely, beautifully cared for—evidently those of a lady and one who had known nothing of hard work.

They chatted gaily and of all sorts of things, taking for granted that Gene had explained everything. How musical her voice was, with its rich cadences! She surely came of some Southern race! Her full white teeth gleamed through dark-red lips. At dinner (and there had been no question of allowing her to dine alone after one glance at that lovely, saddened face) she proved a charming talker. She spoke of well-known books, had met some of the authors and had many tales to tell of them; yet how sad and tragic her face was when quiet.

They had their coffee in the little parlor. She did not seem to want to talk about herself, and the girls were too well bred and had known too much of sorrow to question her. At ten o'clock the Duke arose. "Will you come to the studio, Tessa? I am sorry we cannot have you here to-night, but the flat is very small and we quite fill it. But my studio you will find warm and cozy and my couch will make an excellent bed." She rose and said, " good-night," paused a moment, smiled almost tearfully and added, " you are very good to me."

They went out and down and across the street to the
studio, where the light from a yellow lamp threw grotesque
shadows on the walls of the plaster casts of famous statues

that adorned the room. A white curtain waved gently in
the breeze which came from the open door, and incense
pervaded the air. All was nicely arranged, for the girls
had enjoyed bringing order out of the artistic confusion
to honor the guest, and the Duke found no fault as she
glanced around. "You won't mind those gray covers? They

are my models." With a quick turn she faced Tessa.
"Will you pose for me? You are very beautiful." Tessa
raised her hand in protest and a pleading look on her face
seemed to ask the Duke to cease, but that young woman only
smiled and added: "Just what I have dreamed of to complete my reclining statue of Night. You shall see it in the
morning, and then if only I can copy you! Good-night,
pleasant dreams." She held out her large, brown hand,
and Tessa put her small, white one in it for a moment.
"We shall be good friends," she said, "I feel it, good-
night. Breakfast at eight," she added as she closed
the door, "we shall wait for you." As she descended the
steps she heard the bolt slip, and a moment's pause at
the outer door was long enough for her to hear a fall on
the couch and a heavy sigh.

Breakfast was over; the girls had
gone, each to her own work, and the
Duke and Tessa were in the studio.
The Duke lit a fire in the open grate, put
on her soft, heelless shoes and red fez
cap. Then catching hold of a long cover
she swung it off with a great wave of
her strong arms. Then a damp cloth or
so came away, and there lay, in its
crude state, a fair woman, with
beautiful proportions, on a tiger
skin. Tessa rose and looked at it, and the yellow clay of
the nude body seemed very life-like. "Will you pose for
this for me? If you will I shall be famous." The hazel
eyes looked at the sculptor; through and through they
looked. A moment's thought. Could she do it for art?
Would it be lack of modesty? Was she taking advantage

of her necessity? The thought died under the Duke's honest gaze. "Yes," she breathed, "if you want me." "One thing more." "You will take your meals with us, sleep here, and I will pay you for posing while I model you."

She bowed; her sensitive nature seemed hurt by the business transaction. She disappeared for a few minutes behind a heavy, red curtain, while the Duke arranged a couch and tiger skin on a platform some three feet above the floor. "I am ready," the musical voice said," and Tessa appeared. The Greek proportions, and the dark hair which descended to her waist made one think of Godiva. She ascended the platform and for a moment looked at the clay model, and then instinctively assumed the pose, her head on her arm. How well her dark hair looked on the tiger's head! The Duke seized clay and modeling tools and worked in a frenzy of inspiration. So the hours flew by. Lunchtime came. Tessa had been quiet all the morning and the sculptor too busy to talk. They parted to meet at dinner. The Duke grew interested as she worked to know more of this beautiful creature. Evidently an aristocrat. How she retired into herself and kept out of one's way!

Time rolled on and the model was about complete, and the Duke knew it was her *chef-d'œuvre*, though no critic had yet seen it. The day was sunny and she was putting telling touches here and there to complete her work. A straggling ray of sunlight fell athwart Tessa's face and she looked up and smiled as the Duke stepped back to get a better view. "Will you listen to me while I tell you a tale?" The sculptor laid down a lump of clay she had been using, came over and sat down on the side of the couch. Tessa had rolled herself in a crimson-silk blanket. "You are like that ray of sunlight," she began, "and I am glad I have been of use to you." "You have made my reputation," said the sculptor impulsively. "It is you! I have only copied you!" They had somehow grown to respect and trust each other in these long hours of work.

Tessa continued: "I was born of a noble family in Italy, though I have never lived there since I was a child, for my father moved to Russia when I was but three years of age. My real name is Cármen Felicitas Romero. I do not remember my mother, for she died while I was an infant, but I never missed her care, for my father was so tender and gentle and loving. He simply idolized me and I never knew him to cross a single wish until he objected to the constant attentions of Thaddeus Romanoff.

"Thaddeus was the son of our nearest neighbor, and I think I have always loved him. I remember that before I learned to talk Russian I used to watch with delight the little boy, with mischievous eyes, who sat in church with his nurse on the high-backed bench opposite.

"As a girl I saw him but little, for we lived in the country, and nine miles of forest lay between the estates. When I was fourteen, father sent me to Italy to study, and gave up his interests to live with me in Florence, but when I was sixteen, I took the fever, and the physicians ordered me back to Russia.

"It was about this time that young Thaddeus Romanoff came down to his country estate to spend a few weeks. We lived many miles from St. Petersburg, but even into our remote district strange rumors had penetrated concerning the gay and dissipated life he had been leading; while some people even hinted that he was concerned in certain Nihilistic plots that had been filling the countryside with apprehension.

"We met one day in church, and I was conscious that a pair of bright eyes followed my every movement. Father had told me of Thaddeus' expected visit, or I should never have recognized my childish acquaintance in the tall, soldierly man who bowed so reverently as I passed on my way out. The next day we met in the woods, and although I had quite made up my mind not to speak, I could not resist the winning smile with which he offered me his hand. After this we saw each other frequently, and in a few short weeks we made the discovery that we loved each other. It was then that I insisted that he should come to see me openly, for I could not bear the thought of deceiving my father; but from the first he regarded Thaddeus with a coldness and aversion that seemed to me simply unaccountable.

"Matters went on in this way for several weeks, when one day Thaddeus sent me a note asking me to meet him at nine that night. I went, for I felt that there was some vague trouble ahead, and I had scarcely reached our trysting-place when Thaddeus came galloping up on his mad, black horse.

"He looked pale when he took me in his arms, and in a moment he told me all. He had become implicated in a political conspiracy—he did not have time to give details —but he must fly from Russia at once, and did I have the courage to go with him? I was horrified, and begged for time to think, but he said no—every moment was precious —he might be arrested and exiled at any time without a hearing. I was young—I loved him—he was in trouble and so I went. I remember that we rode to a distant post town and were married, and not until the ceremony was over did I notice that I still wore my slippers and little evening gown of white, and that the wind had loosened my curls to their full length, for I wore no hat. I never thought of my father until we were safely on the vessel and had started for America, and then such a rush of sorrow and shame came over me that for days I refused to be comforted. I never wrote home." Tessa's eyes grew misty, but she struggled bravely on.

"We came to America, settled in San Francisco, and Thaddeus quickly found a comfortable position. At first it was all sunshine and happiness—what did I care for lost grandeur. And my little baby girl was the pride and joy of my life. But one dreadful day a strange woman came to see me. She was a peasant. How can I tell you?"—and Tessa covered her face. "She claimed to be Thaddeus' wife! and said she had followed him to this country. I waited until he came home. I asked him—and oh, the agony on his face! 'I thought her dead,' was all he uttered. I never reproached him." (Tessa was crying now.) I simply left that night—you know the rest—I came direct to Chicago." "And your baby?" the Duke cried. Tessa's face darkened. "I am almost afraid to tell you." "No, no," pleaded the Duke. "Well—my little Cármen is just a block away." "What! in Chicago! And you never told us! Why Tessa—and you might have had her with you all the time!" "Do you really mean that?" she cried with a heavenly smile illuminating her face. "Then I must tell you all about her. Every night after you went back to the flat, I locked the studio and rushed over to see my baby. I didn't dare to tell you about her for fear of losing the income that supported us both; but, oh, I am so glad that you know it now," and her eyes were again suffused with tears.

The next day there was a great surprise in the flat, for when Marjorie and Gene entered the dining-room they found, seated at the table, in her high chair and quite alone,  the dearest, happiest little mite of humanity they had ever seen. After Tessa and the Duke came out from behind the screen and rescued the baby from being smothered with kisses, they explained her appearance and there was a merry-making all round. Little Cármen proved to be the sweetest-tempered child in existence, and spent her days playing on the floor of the studio, while the girls worked or chatted.

Sometimes the baby herself posed as a model, much to the delight of all concerned, and she soon found her way into all the girls' hearts.

But despite little Cármen's cheering presence, Tessa still continued sad. Sometimes she looked so frail that we worried about her, but we knew of nothing that we could do to relieve her anxiety, though we all tried to find her some permanent occupation.

One afternoon Tessa and the Duke were in the studio (the baby was asleep) and Tessa had been posing for the last time for the statue, which was about finished, when the Duke happened to notice a sudden pallor which overspread her face. "Are you ill, dear? You look so tired," Great circles had come under Tessa's eyes. "May I get you some wine?" She ran to her little emergency-shelf and poured some into a tumbler, but before she could turn she heard a fall.

There she lay on the floor—the tiger skin on the platform above her, its eyes glaring into her glassy ones like some horrible fate. How beautiful she was. The Duke stooped and touched her breast ; it was cold and damp.

With a feeling of awe, and reverence, and horror, she

"SOMETIMES THE BABY POSED AS A MODEL."

drew the crimson blanket over the lovely form and went for help.

* * * * * * *

After Tessa's swoon and the Duke's fright we held a consultation as to what we should do, and it was decided that Gene should write to Tessa's father in far-away Russia. Quick as cable could carry it came the reply, and in a few short weeks a grand old man arrived, with snow-white hair and beard, and warm hazel eyes very like Tessa's own. But I shall not attempt to describe the reconciliation!

Many months have passed since then, but the Duke has received happy letters from Tessa, who is improving in health every day.   Only last week came a sweet picture of little Cármen—who has almost grown out of our remembrance—but the young mother who holds her so lovingly in her arms will always be to us " Our Tessa."

CHAPTER XI.

THE DINNER.

HEN the second session of the World's Columbian Commission was almost ended we invited a few of our particular friends to dine with us. There was the courtly Commissioner from Tennessee, the gallant Colonel from Texas, the genial representative from Arkansas, and the eloquent Kentuckian. We put our heads together and arranged an elaborate bill of fare, congratulating ourselves upon the fact that it was absolutely no trouble to give a dinner when we had so excellent a cook as Katie. Alas, when we met at luncheon, we were told that Katie had received news of an accident in her family, and had left suddenly for the country. However, being a faithful creature, she promised to send us a friend who could even rival her in the serving of a meal. Marjorie seemed a little nervous over this friend, and her appearance— for she arrived before we left the house—did not comfort us. She was a short, stout Irish woman, who carried her nose up in the air and seemed continually on the aggressive. When questioned as to her ability as a cook, she replied shortly that she certainly would not pretend to do a thing she knew nothing about, whereupon we hastily retired from the kitchen, and held a

council, which resulted in the Duke's promising to make the salad, Marjorie to set the table, and I was to order the dessert from Kinsley's and send home some flowers. The question as to who was to wait on the table must be settled immediately, so we again went in a body to the kitchen, Marjorie and I following the Duke, who stalked boldly out with her hands in those wonderful pockets. As we opened the kitchen door Bridget was rubbing a pan with a concentrated force and violence that might have been expended on a worthier cause. She did not deign to notice us until the Duke asked if she ever waited on a table. "Indeed, and she waited upon

"LITTLE MARY"

nobody, and all the respectable families she had ever lived out with had 'reached' for themselves." Concluding that argument was useless, and not wishing the Commissioners to do the "reaching" on this occasion, we decided to call in our emergency maid, little Mary, the fourteen-year-old daughter of our washerwoman. Marjorie promised to return early and give her some instructions, and also see that her wardrobe should not reflect discredit on the flat. Feeling assured of Marjorie's ability to rise to the occasion—for she had the most remarkable faculty of making a success of everything she undertook —we parted for the afternoon, promising to return early.

I hastened home at five o'clock to dress, and in answer to my impatient ring the door was opened by little Mary, who was resplendent in a dainty fluted apron and jaunty cap, while her face was so eager and she appeared so anxious to fill her position of trust creditably that I could not help feeling confidence in her ability. A sense of good cheer and welcome pervaded the flat, and the entire suite of rooms wore a holiday air. I could hear rapid walking and the noise of bureau drawers being opened and shut in the Duke's room, and knew from the commotion that the young woman was making an elaborate toilet. Marjorie was a picture in her dainty lavender gown, which suited so well her golden hair, and with a white rose on her breast she seemed the idyllic hostess that we find in the poetry of an age that is gone. She was just putting the finishing touches to the table as I entered the dining-room, and under her artistic hand it was a combination of dazzling cut-glass, shining silver, soft lights and glowing flowers. Vases of chrysanthemums stood on the sideboard, and the mantel was covered with roses and trailing vines. In the center of the table was a tall, slender Bohemian glass vase, the pride of the flat, filled with La France roses and feathery Maiden Hair ferns, while long fern-leaves were laid on the table around the vase.

Marjorie had just trailed a piece of ivy around one of the tall silver candelabra, when she turned and saw me. "Oh, Gene, I have just been wishing for you. Do run upstairs and return the courtesy of our frying-pan, which we loaned Mrs. Brown, by borrowing her oyster forks." I assented and soon returned, not only with the

oyster forks, but with Mrs. Brown herself, who followed me
and bore in her hand an immense, many-pronged silver
épergne. " You dear girls, giving a dinner and didn't tell
me? Here I've brought you my épergne. It belonged
to my grandfather, Colonel Carey, of Virginia, and we
used to have it on our table when my first husband and I
entertained so much in Baltimore. Trouble me? Not a
bit in the world. I can whisk all those things off in a
jiffy." And the good-natured, but misguided woman,
suiting the action to the word, seized upon poor Marjorie's artistic decorations and swept them ruthlessly from
the table, planting her huge, ungainly ornament triumphantly in their place. And there it stood on our little table,
looking about as inappropriate as a silk hat on a three-
year-old boy. In vain we protested, but she, still insist-
ing, carried her disagreeable point. We continued the
preparations, and just as soon as she had taken her departure—and she stayed until we were beside ourselves—
Marjorie, in anything but a sweet spirit, laid violent hands
upon the relic of Carey elegance, and transplanted it to
the kitchen table. The New York cousin, whom we had
asked to chaperone our party, came first, and was simply
charming in her gray dress and pink roses, and we were
exceedingly proud of her as she entered the room in her
gracious, elegant way. "She is so very swell, you know,"
the Duke said.

By this time little Mary had reached a state of nervous
excitement which was appalling to behold, while Bridget
was calling on every saint in the calendar known to a de-
vout Catholic, but in spite of these minor domestic frictions
Bridget had prepared a well-cooked dinner, and we seated
ourselves at the table with a sense of relief that everything
so far had been successful.

Our guests were exceedingly entertaining, and told a number of amusing incidents about the first meeting of the Commissioners. A certain very small Commissioner, who seemed to amuse them greatly, had always carried an im-

mense palm-leaf fan, and when he arose to his feet to demand the floor, he would wave his fan violently at the president to compel his attention, knowing that he would not otherwise be recognized. An incident was divertingly related showing that there was still a strong feeling exist-

ing among certain of the Southern Commissioners. Upon
one occasion Mr. Wilson, Republican Commissioner from
Connecticut, had the chair and was enumerating the various States whose Legislatures had failed to make any appropriation. When he mentioned Georgia, the Commissioner from that State, an unreconstructed rebel and a
Democrat, immediately pricked up his ears. The ex-Gov-
ernor, very old and exceedingly deaf, is in addition so
rheumatic that walking is both painful and difficult. Catching the one word, "Georgia," and being suspicious of the
friendly feeling existing in the heart of a Republican from
Connecticut, besides, being totally unable to hear a word,
he excitedly seized the arms of his chair, and with sup-
pressed groans, raised himself to his feet. Clutching his
cane, he laboriously stamped across the room to where Mr.
Colquitt, of Tennessee, was sitting. "Colquitt, what is that
man saying about Gawjah?" he asked in a loud whisper,
while he looked threateningly at the chair. "Oh, nothing,
Governor, nothing. He's only referring to the fact that
Georgia, with other States, has failed to make an appropriation," Mr. Colquitt answered reassuringly. "Well, tell him
that I say," and the Governor shook his cane threateningly,
"to let Gawjah alone. It's none of his business what our
Legislature does, and if he don't like what I say, tell him
that I am here to answer for the honah of Gawjah, suh!"
and the irate old gentleman turned and stamped back to his
seat, where he sat glaring at the chair during the re-
mainder of the afternoon. We all laughed very heartily at
this story, and no one seemed more amused than the Commissioner who had related it, as he always thoroughly en-
joys his own jokes.

Our dinner was progressing famously. The soup had

been delicious, the turkey beautifully done, and I was secretly wondering at little Mary's aptitude, when I happened to glance at Marjorie, who was regarding her with painful uneasiness. I soon discovered that our small maidservant, in her zeal, not only removed the plates with each course, but the salt, the olives, the almonds, the celery and the glasses. These things were placed on the sideboard for an instant, and then returned to the table, the glasses being studiously emptied and refilled each time. I had my misgivings as to the capacity of the ice-pitcher under such trying circumstances, and far from feeling Marjorie's annoyance, was highly amused, as all the signals given were in vain. Little Mary was at that moment about to swoop down on the Duke's glass, but that young woman was too quick for her, and held it firmly while she turned to the Commissioner next to her, saying : " Now, Major, tell us one of your good stories," and without further urging he told of a recent experience.

Being invited last spring to attend the house-warming of an elegant home on the South Side, owned by one of Chicago's wealthy pork-packers, he had accepted and enjoyed the evening thoroughly. When the time came for him to take his departure he bade his hostess good-night, and she accompanied him to the door, where stood a tall, red-faced Irishman in a dress suit, to whom she said : " John, won't you call Major G.'s carriage ? " The man started out of the front door followed by the Commissioner, and as it was an exceedingly stormy night, the Major stood under the shelter of the porte cochère, saying : " John, I will wait here until you find the carriage." John, in the meantime, hatless and with thin shoes, went out across the lawn, found the carriage, and came back for our friend, whom he politely assisted down the steps. "Imagine my surprise and mortification," added the narrator of this story, "when, upon the following evening, I saw my hostess in her box at the opera with the man whom I had mistaken for her footman sitting beside her. I congratulated myself every time I looked at that box that my overcoat had been so tightly buttoned that I could not reach my pocket, and that so I had been spared the mortification of tipping my host for his courtesy."

By this time we had finished the more substantial part of our dinner, and were waiting for dessert. Little Mary had retired to the kitchen, and we heard an ominous pounding and commotion out there. I suspected that Bridget was having difficulty with something, and when little Mary finally appeared with the ice cream, I knew that it must have been the mould that had confused her, as there was no shape to the cream whatever. Marjorie whispered the one word "cake," and little Mary again disappeared, while we all three talked at once, on entirely different subjects, and our pretty chaperone smiled sweetly on the guests to cover up this domestic difficulty. Our hand-maid at last returned, and with a frightened face, said to Marjorie in an audible whisper: "It's fell in the chute." Of course we tried to look unconscious, but the expression on the face of the Commissioner from Arkansas was too much for us. He seemed anxious and curious and amazed all at once over little Mary's message, and fearing that he would think our cake the victim of some kind of a rifle match, we hastened to explain to him that all flats have chutes, leading from the kitchen to the basement, where ashes and various things can be deposited. The covering to our shute had been broken, and Bridget had doubtless carelessly set the cake-basket on this broken lid and it had gone through.

In spite of our embarrassment over this accident, it made us all laugh so heartily that we drank our coffee in a right merry mood, and after our guests had gone, and we sat about the fire talking it all over, as girls will, we congratulated ourselves upon the fact that our little dinner had been quite a success. " But, girls, did you hear the sequel to Mrs. Brown's épergne ? " Marjorie said. " Well, you know, Virginia, that I set it on the kitchen table in my wrath and vexation, and little Mary tells me it perfectly infuriated Bridget, as it took up so much room—you know, girls, it does look like a steamboat—so she pushed it under the sink out of her way, and who should come around to the kitchen door and see it but Mrs. Brown herself!" "Served her right," said the Duke, "we never do have a thing in this flat but she wants to have the entire management of it all." "From frying-pans on up to épergnes," Marjorie added, laughingly.

S we were sitting around the fire one evening after dinner, the girls said: "Now, Virginia, do tell us about Lady Aberdeen; is she as lovely as they say?"

"Indeed she is! I am completely charmed with her."

"When did you see her?" queried the Duke.

"When she accepted Mrs. Palmer's invitation to visit the Board rooms of the Lady Managers."

"Is she handsome?"

"She is tall and fine-looking, with a very intelligent face and a pair of earnest gray eyes. She seemed much interested in the Board of Lady Managers, and was anxious to know if Sir Henry Wood had yet nominated the committee of women in England, who were to co-operate with our Board. We told her we had not heard of it, and Sir Henry had scarcely had time to arrange a committee, as he had only sailed from New York on the fifth of October. She thinks it best, as there is a separate commission of men for Ireland, Scotland and England, that there should also be a

separate commission of women, as the articles exhibited by
women in each country would be so entirely different.
Mrs. Palmer suggested that she should work that matter up
upon her return to England.

"While we were talking, a gentleman called to see Mrs.
Palmer in regard to having Belique ware manufactured
upon the World's Fair
grounds during the
Exposition, and I
think they have de-
cided that the Belique
manufactory which he
represented will con-
tribute a vase de-
signed and made
entirely by women, to
the Woman's build-
ing.

"Before she left the
office Mrs. Stark-
weather asked Lady
Aberdeen to inscribe
her name upon our
autograph book, and
she smilingly wrote,

LADY ABERDEEN.

'Ishbel Aberdeen, Haddo House, Scotland.' As she
returned the pen she said: 'I imagine you have few such
unusual names ; and do you know that Ishbel is the Gaelic
for Elizabeth ?'

"In her sweet, womanly way, Lady Aberdeen talked to us
about our great work here for women, which she thought
so fine, and her presence was so gracious and winning that

she quite won our hearts. She told Mrs. Palmer that she thought the English women were far in advance of the American women in a political way, and referred to the recent article upon that subject by Justin McCarthy, in the *North American Review*, as a very correct presentation of the wonderful influence wielded by women in English politics.

" 'But,' said her ladyship, 'I am convinced that in a business way the American woman is far ahead of the English. We have no such system of bookkeeping and office work as I see here among your women.' "

" Gene, I should think that you would see many interesting and queer people in the Board rooms. Why don't you put them down in a diary ?"

"Why, I have a little note book," said Gene, "it is somewhere in my room," and she soon returned with a much worn little memorandum book.

" That is great," said the Duke ; " now read us some of the extracts in it."

" Won't it bore you ?"

"Of course not."

" Well, here is one :"

Nov. 23d.—"Now, girls, this is really remarkable " (aside). " Mrs. ——— ———, specialist, has the secret of removing all wrinkles from the face. A queer-looking woman is with her, whom she calls one of her 'samples.' Six months ago, the 'sample' asserts, her face was as wrinkled as a checker-board. It is really quite round and rosy now. The wrinkles are removed by electric needles (which may account for the fact that the pupil in the 'sample's' left eye is three times as large as that in the right), and the process takes three months. The specialist has established a house here where patients may board until cured. She says she will do one eye for anybody free of charge."

" I think John L. Sullivan has made the same assertion,"
said the Duke, sotto voce.

" But, listen now, girls, this is really ridiculous." (Reads.)

" The specialist's idea of an exhibit is this: She will take
some old lady, the older and more wrinkled the better, and
removing the wrinkles from one side of her face, will exhibit her in the Woman's Building."

" Only a full-fledged voter would have the strength of
mind to do that," said Marjorie aside.

" The old lady thus exhibited will have the wrinkles removed from the other side of her face after the Exposition, the entire treatment in this case to be free of charge."

"'The only suggestion I would make," said the Duke,
who was convulsed with laughter, "is this; that the old lady
keep turning her head from side to side like a Chinese
Mandarin, showing first one side and then the other."

"Now, you needn't laugh girls, for what I have read you
actually occurred."

" Do read some more," came in chorus from the girls, who
were highly amused.

" Well, here is a second extract, if you care to hear it."

Nov. 24th.—" I was sitting at my desk this morning,
when the door opened and a little old lady glided softly in.
She wore a bonnet like a candle-snuffer, with the strings
tied down straight over her ears, while three black ostrich
feathers, guiltless of all curl, stood straight up in front.
She was small and thin and held a black shawl tightly
around her with one hand, while she grasped a little black
bag with the other. I think she would have called this bag
a reticule. She wore large, owlish-looking glasses, and fix-
ing her piercing eyes on me said in a deep, bass voice : ' I
am a Daughter of the Revolution.

errand to me, which in spite of her terrible voice, was a very mild one."

"Here is another entry, girls, of the same date, which will make your blood run cold. It is almost too horrible to relate, but as it is a matter of history, I think I will tell you. Mr. Hirst, Chief of Installation, sent down a letter to-day, in accordance with Mrs. Palmer's request that he would notify her of all

"'My grandfather was in the Revolutionary War, and so was my father.'

"As she peered at me through those horned glasses and looked so fierce, she added in a deep voice:

"'All my family have been fighters."

"Cold chills ran down my back at that announcement, but I arose and offered her a seat, and she stated her applications made by women, announcing the fact that a certain woman, an embalmer by profession——"

"A what?" screamed the Duke.

"An embalmer. Now listen, and if you don't say that the Lady Managers have a queer collection of letters, I will be surprised. She wishes to exhibit her work, and adds that she desires to compete—think of it ! She says in a very matter-of-fact, business-like way, that she wants a corpse constantly on exhibition in the Woman's Building."

"Oh Gene, that is horrible ; read us something else," said Marjorie.

"Well, I merely read it to let you see what queer people there are in the world."

"The Duke arose and came over and stood by Gene, reading over her shoulder.

"There is something interesting ! Read that."

"Yes, that may amuse you, as it is an anecdote that a Presbyterian minister told me one day, when he came in the office on business.

"A young man before his marriage said to his fiancée : 'I don't think we ought to have any secrets between us, and so I will tell you that I am a somnambulist.' 'Oh, that is of no consequence," said she. "I am a Presbyterian, and am willing to go half-way with you.' "

"Of course Gene would remember that little Presbyterian joke," said the Duke, laughing.

"Well ! I have only one more entry now to read :

Nov. 30th.—"A letter received by the Board of Lady Managers to-day, stated that the writer would be pleased to place an elevator of aluminum in the Woman's Building, for use during the Exposition, adding :

"'Though it seems presumptuous for a humble man like

me to attempt the elevation of woman, the crown of crea-
tion.' Now, is not that gallant for a business letter?"

"Is that all you have written?" said the Duke.

Just then the front door was opened by Katie, and Mr.
Middleton came in with a radiant face and a few American
Beauties for Gene.

Marjorie and the Duke soon withdrew from the parlor,
and as they sat by the dining-room lamp, the Duke said:

"Did you notice, Marjorie, how Virginia blushed when
Mr. Middleton was announced? I'm very much afraid
that there is a romance brewing under our very eyes."

"Well! Jack Middleton is a true, loyal fellow, and I
have always liked him," Marjorie answered; "but I am not
afraid that we will lose Gene, for having had so much
attention she is really over fastidious, and will not be very
easily won."

CHAPTER XIII.

JACKSON PARK, BY THE DUKE.

ONE never realizes as one lives the days away how much of poetry and romance, beauty and interest, there are in the twenty-four hours.

A month's work in the modeling-shops in Jackson Park afforded many pleasant memories and much knowledge of men. A woman's advent among them was a matter of less interest, perhaps owing to the fact that almost all the workers were foreigners, and abroad it is not so unusual for women to do industrial work. A quiet corner had been apportioned to the Danish sculptor and his wife, and there my model was set up. The modeling-shop was a mere temporary building, long and low, and the midsummer sun kept the thermometer way up in the nineties.

The decorative work for several of the buildings of the Columbian Exposition was being done here, and a hundred men were seeking expression for genius, or daily pay for daily food. The early morning always found in his place the tall, dark, curly-haired German, picturesque in his white blouse with red collar, broad leather belt with big buckle and his short brier-wood pipe between his teeth. On the scaffolding in front of his " Goddess of Electricity," he moved constantly, his white cap a star against the gray

wall. Two spandrels covered the arch dividing the modeling from the casting department, and on these worked the
only American who had found occupation in the shops.
Tall, slender, nervous, truly American in all his movements,
he would model a bit, descend from his ladder, step back

to look at his work
and then rush mad-
ly to make some
change.

Perhaps no more
earnest worker con-
nected with all the
big fair could be
found than the little
lad whose willing
feet and active
hands did all my
bidding. In the field
of sculpture he
hoped to earn a liv-
ing for a large fam-
ily of brothers and
sisters, and after a
day's mechanical
work in waiting on
me, he studied at night in the Art School. Often he
would bring me a model to correct which he had made;
and then how his eyes would brighten and his cheeks glow at
a word of praise!—and I doubt if Giotto felt more inspired
than he, surrounded by the spirit of art and fired by ambi-
tion. His great, sad eyes, pallid face and ragged clothes,
recalled Murillo's fancies in old Spain.

In this rude shop a vivid imagination found ample play, and the big, strong fellows who carried buckets of plaster for casting, or the dreamy artists whose thoughts were far away, each had some theme for story. As I worked I wondered what the motive of each life might be.

One afternoon the whistle had just sounded to renew work, when I saw coming towards me a man below the medium height, with long red-brown hair, deep sunken blue-black eyes and a long, drooping mustache. In his hand he held a large sombrero and from his shoulders a military cape depended. A flannel shirt, a gaudy tie and a brilliant scarf around his waist completed a most unusual costume. A model, evidently, and a character! He threw his hair back with his hand, looked up at me where I stood at work, and handed me a card on which was written  "Leon Lubrowoski," musician—model. "You want a model I understand?" "Yes," I replied. He looked like Charles I in a cowboy's dress, and I wondered for what I could use him. I resolved mentally to make a character study of him. "For what have you posed?" "A villain," and as he stuck his hat on the back of his head and folded his arms he looked it. "A Spanish cavalier, a monk, Christ, Mephistophéles—anything, everything."

"Do you make a living by playing, also, and on what?"
"The violin, but I never take money for it. It is my love
and my pleasure." His answer excited my curiosity and I
questioned him further. "What country do you come
from?" "Poland. I have been here six years. I am a
vegetarian. For eight years I have eaten nothing cooked. I
live on fruit and berries; meat excites one, and I never get
excited; you could not make me angry—I think coolly,
I drink nothing but water, nor do I smoke. When one
lives on fruit one loses all desire for such things—also the
mind is clearer; not hampered by food and body." "Can
you do much work without meat?" I asked. "Yes, providing it is not too great physicial exertion. The world
spends its time in making a living and dies before it does
the living. Now life is worth enough to take time to enjoy
and to cultivate what God has given you; not laboring all
day long, eating and sleeping—that is animal existence;
not life." "What pleasures do you indulge in?" I asked.
"Reading and music I like best; metaphysics, political
economy and theosophy. Tinsley, Huxley, Adams and
Darwin, Lubbock's 'Pleasures of Life,' all have references
in them to other books; and those I buy. I have a library
of about two hundred and fifty volumes; I pose and make
enough to eat and wear; fifteen cents gets a supply of
apples sufficient for a day; eating fruit does away with the
necessity of preparing meals and washing cooking utensils,
and gives more time to read and conduces to freedom.
No, I never drink milk; men have made slaves of cows and
I believe in freedom for all; men are slaves themselves to
raising cattle. I don't believe in marriage as it at present
exists. A woman married is a slave to her husband. How
can she wash and cook and care for the children and be

free to think? She wants pleasures as well as a man, and if she has to do drudgery, she can't think and enjoy life. All should be free to enjoy themselves; to be happy and to make others so."

That this curious subject, a philosopher in rags, posed for me, I need hardly say; and the sketch, like the model, could not be named, for in it were ideas and their contradictions.

The bell rang—the day was done. We put down our tools, doffed caps and aprons, and filed out of the shop. Across the park, over the sand and timber we went, forming part of the black line of wage-earners, crawling like ants, toward the gate. Each going home to some one he loved—each with his life with its joy and pain—real to him and not existing for the man beside him; striving, toiling, patiently enduring, making a living, and as my philospher model said: "Dying before he did the living."

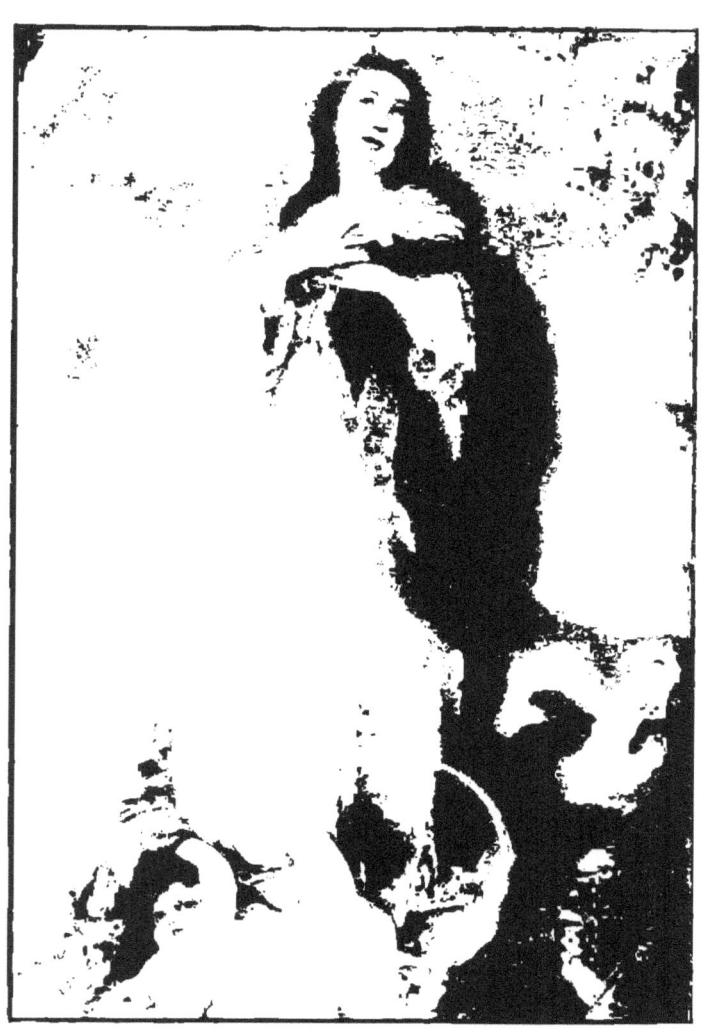

CHAPTER XIV.

CHRISTMAS.

My Dear Will:—How kind you were to remember the flat with that splendid bag of game! We all enjoyed it immensely, and I wish you could have been with us at our Christmas dinner, although we did come near having an accident afterwards. We had been having a very exciting day, the bell ringing every other moment, and all sorts of mysterious packages coming in, for everyone was so good to us. We seemed to be having a regular donation party, and it all commenced last October when Mrs. Peabody, of Evanston, who has always been the loyal friend of the flat, sent us the great basket of goodies from what she called her farm. It was her crab-apple jelly with the Oriental flavor of the rose-leaf in it that you liked so much when you took dinner with us on your way through the city.

Then came a beautiful box from Louisville, filled with brandied peaches that the Duke's mother sent us ; and last, but not least, the contribution from that sweet Mrs. Gould, of Moline, a member of the Board of Lady Managers, who sent us such a big box on Thanksgiving, filled with preserves and jellies and pickles, and on top of them all, inside of the cover, a mass of orange and white feathery

chrysanthemums from her own garden.   Who but a woman
would have thought of that last artistic touch?   I don't
need to tell you what a help this has been in our housekeeping, for with all that we can do, it is more expensive
than boarding, and none of us can afford to spend all the
money we make on the flat.   Gene, you know, is taking
vocal lessons, and the Duke is saving up money for her
art studies abroad, and as for me, you know how heavy
my expenses have always been, and more than ever this
winter, since I have taken up so many studies outside of
my work.   But I am straying rather far from the subject
of Christmas.

It was Gene's birthday, so we made a double holiday of it,
and gave a pretty dinner to which we invited her very best

friends.   The Duke and I had managed
the whole thing as a surprise, so that
Gene did not know we had remembered that it was her birthday until
Katie brought in the great cake, with
its twenty-two candles all lighted.   We
had spent nearly all the morning deco-
rating the dining-room while Gene was
at church.   (She did not go alone.)   And
the result surpassed our wildest expectations, for the Duke
has the most exquisite taste.   First, we had the janitor bring
up from our store-room in the cellar, the big round top
which we always use on our little table on state occasions.
Then, while Katie laid the cloth, the Duke disappeared in the
back hall, returning in triumph with the dearest little Christmas tree in the world.   The girls exclaimed with delight (for
Carrie and Vinnie and Maude were with us), and we all set
to work with a will.   We placed it in the center of the table

and trimmed it with golden threads of tinsel, hanging upon it all the smaller toys that we had bought for little Mary's brother and sister, and for the janitor's children, for we had asked them all in for dinner at seven (our own was at five), and for a frolic afterward. On the table under the spreading branches, we grouped the larger toys, and at a happy suggestion from Carrie, we sifted bits of fleecy white cotton all over our little tree until it looked like one of Lowell's pines " that wore ermine too dear for an earl."

After this, we festooned strings of Japanese lanterns of quaintest shapes from the chandelier in the center to the

four corners of the room, and fastened several spike-edged palm leaves in a graceful row above the sideboard. The effect of all this decoration was certainly gay and pretty enough to please the most fastidious, but the Duke stood critically on one side of the table with her brows knitted, and with a preoccupied air that we have all learned to know and respect, as the herald of some bright suggestion. Suddenly she exclaimed: " I have it," rushed into the kitchen, returning with Katie and an enormous step ladder, which we had bought in the early days of our housekeeping be-

fore we had accustomed ourselves to our diminutive home.
She had noticed the reflections of the table with its tree in
the mirrors belonging to the mantel and sideboard at the
opposite sides of the room, and it had occurred to her to
introduce a third glass which would reflect an added brilliancy when the candles were lighted.   It was the work of
a moment to get a great round, old-fashioned mirror from
her own room and hang it opposite the table, but unfortu-
nately the framework was of dark wood, while our little
dining-room is all in oak.   Someone suggested holly, and
so we wreathed the entire mirror with the glossy leaves
and the red berries, tho' it was hard work to drive the pins
into the unyielding wood, especially as we had to use hair
brushes for hammers, as this article was not included in
the inventory of our household belongings.   After this we
brought in from the parlor the long jardinière, with its row
of fresh vines and bright-colored geraniums, and placed it
under the mirror, but even then our critical artist was not
satisfied, for on each side of the glass was a space of two
or three feet that showed the light wall-paper.

Again the Duke knitted her brows, and again we kept
silence, and in a few minutes our old black Japanese
screen, with its golden birds, was impressed into service;
but there was yet the other side, and well we knew that
there was not an extra curtain in the flat, as weeks before
it had depleted the family pocket-book to hang portières
in each door.   The case seemed hopeless, but our artist
had another inspiration, and in a moment had hung
up Gene's crimson opera cloak by one corner so that the
graceful fur-edged folds fell into place, and lo, the effect
was magical.   A gleaming circle wreathed in holly and
drooping with vines and flowers stood out from a dark, in-

discriminate background and reflected again and again the
table with its dainty appointments and snow-laden tree.

The only lights we used that night were the lanterns,
and the candles on tree   and table, and as our
friend from Maine declared   on seeing it, the din-

ing-room had undergone as much of a transformation as
Aladdin's palace.

Punctually at five our guests arrived, and one and all
exclaimed at our new banqueting hall. The dinner progressed with mirth and jollity, for we had the old-fashioned
bonbons on the table, and pulled the snappers just like

children. I cannot tell you how pretty the girls all looked
in the candle-light with their quaint paper caps, or how
becoming the Priscilla hood of white tissue was to dear
Mrs. Starkweather, who was acting as our chaperone.

Our guests were all in the happiest mood, especially our
friend from Maine, who aroused shouts of laughter by
telling, in his inimitable manner, three of his best-known
stories about "old Squire Rawson," when, like an appari-
tion, Mrs. Brown appeared. She did not have the sombre
effect of Banquo's ghost, however, for she carried in both
hands a tarnished silver soup tureen filled with maple syrup,
which she had brought for a Christmas present to the flat.

In her arms were a new pair of red-
topped, copper-toed boots belonging to
Lycurgus, which she had carried in to
show us, while over one shoulder depended a pair of diminutive trousers
which, she assured us, entirely without
embarrassment, were Philander's first,
which she had just made (and here she

STELLA.

heaved a gentle sigh) out of the moth-eaten remnant of
her first husband's wedding suit.

We were drinking our coffee in the parlor after dinner,
when merry voices and heavy little footsteps sounded in
the hall ; a ring came at the door, and Katie ushered in our
little guests, who arrived in a body.

The table had been reset and we had relighted the tree
when they sat down to dinner, and such shy, happy, well-
behaved children I never before saw. Stella, our small
neighbor across the hall, was giving a party, too, and
many of her little friends flocked over to see our children.
Two of the little girls, Daisy and Jean, wore Japanese cos-

tumes, which delighted all the children except poor little red-haired Anthony, who was so frightened that he buried his face in his napkin and howled until he felt the reassuring touch of little Mary's fingers.

After dinner there was a great frolic, and Olga, who doesn't speak a word of English, became so excited that

DAISY AND JEAN.

she got up and spoke a piece, which her older sister gravely assured us was Humpty-Dumpty in Swedish. She rocked back and forth on her wooden shoes as she recited, and the words sounded very odd. They were:

" Lilla bulla soppa kulla,
Trilla neffer kulla.
Ingen mon e detta lon,
Lilla bulla bupta kon."

After this our harper came into the hall below as he always does on holidays, and we invited him in, that the little folks might dance. We had planned to leave them in full possession of the flat under Katie's care, for we were all going down to the Christmas performance of the Messiah by the Apollo Club, to which Gene and I belong, as you know. We had gone to our rooms to get our wraps, and were just about ready to start, when we noticed the smell of smoke, and hearing someone call "Fire!" rushed to the

dining-room. What a sight met our eyes! Our beautiful table was a smoking ruin, while standing over it with a great empty dish-pan in his hand stood Pat, whom Katie calls her "best kimpany." Six of the pretty after-dinner coffee-cups that I had picked up abroad were broken, several napkins were

LITTLE HELEN.   scorched, but worse than all, a great, brown hole was burned through our best tablecloth, through our white felt pad, and marked the pine of our table top. Katie, who had spread the cloth, had tried to make the table especially beautiful, so, in addition to the pad, and underneath the outside layer of damask, she had put four of our best tablecloths.

I saw that Gene could scarcely repress the tears, for she does love a prettily appointed table, and we knew what ruin this meant to our slender stock of linen; but Katie was such a picture of misery that we were all obliged to burst out laughing. We had had an unusually fine dessert that night—a mould of ice cream made in the form of a watermelon, with the German strawberries in the centre, then the layer of ice and finally the outside of green pistache. It had been the pride of Katie's heart and it was the cause of all our misery, for she and Pat were so anxious to finish it before it melted that they had left the table to its fate, and one of the lighted candles had probably fallen from the tree.

In spite of our disaster, however, we reached the Auditorium in time, and it was with the greatest pride that I ushered Gene into her place in the chorus, for she was my new member, and this was her first concert, and I knew that no one could look without pleasure on that sweet, animated face, above the gown of pale blue crêpe. In her hand she carried some gorgeous roses that had been presented by a certain young man, while in her hair glittered an enameled blue butterfly, with opalescent wings, that was the common property of the flat.

We arrived just in time and had gained our places comfortably when the curtain rose and the Auditorium lay before us. I could not begin to tell you how it looks from the stage. The stereotyped description will not fit at all, for though it is the same magnificent hall, with its arches of starry light, yet when you take this point of view and the sea of upturned faces stretches away from you, the effect is to add greatly to its immensity. The tiers of boxes, on either side, were filled with fair women in evening dress, and the softness of coloring in the whole scene could only be likened to some Oriental picture.

But we did not have long to look, for in a moment the spendid Thomas Orchestra, which was to accompany us, touched the opening strains of Handel's magnificent Oratorio.

When I was in London last summer I had the good fortune to hear the Royal Choral Society, with its membership of a thousand voices, singing the Golden Legend, with Nordica, and Albani and Lloyd and Henschel for soloists, with ten thousand people listening in Prince Albert Hall, and with the German Emperor and Empress and all the royalty of England in the boxes ; but I can honestly say that there was no better chorus singing, nor was there one-tenth the enthusiasm that was exhibited at this masterful rendering, under the leadership of Mr. Tomlins, who is respected and admired by all lovers of music, and simply worshiped by his own club.

We reached home at twelve o'clock, tired but happy, with our eventful day, and as I passed the library on my way to my room, I noticed a slender figure, with brown hair under a monk's hood of crimson, standing with a taller shadow ominously near the mistletoe bough ; but of course there was nothing in this, for was it not our independent Gene ?

You must forgive me, dear Will, for writing this very long, and rather commonplace letter ; but I feel a little lonely sometimes, especially on holidays.   Oh, why did you go to Australia ?   MARJORIE.

CHAPTER XV.

THE LITTLE BLUE BUTTERFLY.

WHEN Gene refused to open the large box she received at the breakfast table one sunny April morning, the Duke gave me a very significant glance, for Gene is never selfish, and neither is she afraid of a joke. However, she calmly ignored us on this occasion, and carried the package off to her room, while we lingered over our coffee to discuss the situation. "I'm afraid it may have something to do with that young man who comes every night," declared the Duke. "Oh, nonsense," I replied, "Gene isn't going to do anything precipitate," but nevertheless I had my misgivings, for I had noticed that our ten o'clock rule was being broken with ominous regularity, and only the night before I had preferred taking my book over to the studio with the Duke, to interrupting a very interesting tête-a-tête in the library.

The evening of our conversation in the dining-room one of our neighbors was to give a large party. We had all been invited, but the Duke had to work on one of her models, and I was fathoms deep in the "Chevalier of Pensieri Vani," so we sent our regrets. Gene had decided to go, however, and we went to her room after dinner to assist her to dress. When she had donned her dainty gown of white chiffon, and gathered her pretty bronze hair high on her head, she made a charming picture. "How do I look?" and she turned to the Duke a little defiantly. There was a sparkle and brilliancy about her that was quite enchanting, and a subdued brightness in her glance that was far from commonplace. I looked at her in surprise, but the Duke was not to be conquered by this radiant young beauty. She drew back critically. "Yes, you will do very well, but I wish you had some flowers—you need a bit of color;" and she stepped to the bureau to examine the ornaments in Gene's cushion. "Here, this makes it perfect;" and drawing the little blue butterfly from its resting-place she fastened it among the burnished coils. It certainly was lovely. How well the opalescent tints brought out the lights in her eyes!

Just then a familiar ring was heard at the door, and I rushed out to admit Mr. Middleton. I had never seen him look so distinguished, and he, too, seemed rather exalted. While we were talking in the parlor he asked me casually if Gene had received a box that morning, and smiled with satisfaction at my affirmative reply. Just then she entered; but what was there about that lovely vision to make his face blanch and the light die out of his eyes? And why, when she offered her hand so sweetly in greeting did he ignore it and pretend to be picking up a glove?

Gene, poor child, drew back proudly, but I caught the gleam of a tear that sparkled more brightly than the little jeweled ornament that glinted above it.

After they had gone the Duke and I held an indignation meeting that culminated in nothing more serious than a dainty luncheon and a cup of hot chocolate, which we spread on the low table by the hearth. We waited until the rumble of the carriage announced that the wanderers had returned, and then giving a last touch to the table, and a final thrust at the cannel fire, which made the room blaze with ruddy light and sent the sparks flying up the wide chimney, we escaped to our rooms. But our tempting preparations were in vain, for we heard a formal goodnight at the door, and a moment later the key turned in Gene's room, and no notice had been taken of our little feast. We slipped into the parlor, extinguished the hissing kettle, and removed everything quietly that she might not be wounded by seeing our preparations in the morning, and then we hurried off to bed.

But when the morning came Gene was in no condition to notice our futile efforts, for the Duke found her ill with a violent headache, and made her stay in bed in spite of her protests.

When I returned at night she seemed much better and joined us at dinner, but she appeared listless and heavy-eyed, and the succeeding days brought no change.

One day we heard casually that Mr. Middleton was about to sail for Europe, and so the Duke resolved upon a bold stroke.

We were at dinner—Gene, as usual, making a pretense of eating—when the Duke remarked to me: "Have you heard, Marjorie, that Jack Middleton is going to Europe?" Of course I *had* heard, but Gene hadn't, and as the Duke afterward confessed, she could have bitten her tongue out for having uttered the words, when she saw the stricken look in the poor child's eyes. She tried to smile and say something, but the words would not come. However, she stayed bravely until we finished our coffee, but it was a relief to us all when we heard her lock the door of her room. We went across to the studio where she would not hear us talk, but we could not solve the problem, and as we did not want to leave her long we stayed but a few minutes.

When we returned to the flat Katie let us in, whispering in awe-struck tones: "Mrs. Brown's gone into Miss Fairfax's room, mum." "How did she get in?" demanded the Duke angrily, but stopped when she heard the sobs behind Gene's locked door. "Why, she said she *must* see Miss Fairfax; she knew she hadn't been well, and she wanted to cheer her up, and so I let her knock. Miss Gene wouldn't answer, and so Mrs. Brown went into your room, Miss Marjorie, and got in through the closet door."

The Duke's eyes flashed with indignation, but I thought it might do Gene good to have Mrs. Brown rush in, though we had feared to attempt it.

We sat down quietly in the dining-room, and in a few minutes Mrs. Brown came out wiping her eyes, and with a sweetness and tenderness in her manner that we would not have believed possible. "Yes, girls, she's told me all about it," she said, "and unless there's some mistake that Mr. Middleton ought to be ashamed, for they've never had a single quarrel, and she don't know what's made him angry." Just here she was interrupted by a procession of little boys who came to our back door dragging in Lycurgus, who was protesting with many howls.

"Make him tell what's in that box, ma," cried Thomas Jefferson. "I saw him hiding it under Phil's bed."

"What is in that box, my son?" demanded Mrs. Brown sternly, and the offender, amid bitter tears, removed the string, lifted the cover and revealed—a mass of faded roses. "It came to Miss Fairfax on April Fool's morning," he sobbed, "and I just changed it and sent a box of newspaper instead. I meant to send it back, but I forgot all about it until to-day;" and the miserable infant wept copious floods of tears. His mother leaned forward and with one large hand dealt him a generous cuff on the ear that sent him home yelling, while with the other she plucked a card from among the faded flowers, and handed it to the Duke. It read: "If I may hope, wear one of these roses in your hair to-night."

Nothing was said for a moment, and then Mrs. Brown rose abruptly. "I am going down stairs to telephone," and she disappeared. We didn't exchange a word after she left, but I could hear a French heel tapping the floor impatiently, and I knew by this infallible sign that our Duke was laboring under strong excitement. It was but a moment until Mrs. Brown returned, like young Lochinvar's Ellen, "with a smile on her lip but a tear in her eye." "Yes, girls, I got the telephone number I wanted, and you had better go and take a walk just as quick as you can. I am going home," and she suited the action to the word.

The Duke rose to open the door, and as the good woman passed she threw her arms around her and kissed her good-night.

HE Duke and I walked silently down the Lake Shore Drive. The summer sea smiled before us; a few white-winged ships gave substance to the dreamlike expanse; the Crib seemed floating between two oceans; the sky spread its glory from zenith to horizon, and the shining lake flushed and changed each moment with the rainbow tints of the sunset. As we advanced the glowing crimson paled to ashes of roses, and the rich purple became a faint violet—the day was departing.

We walked to the end of the esplanade and turned to retrace our steps. The shadowy veil of night had hidden the Crib, the ships were phantoms, and lo! there hung in the west a slender sickle of silvery light—the sweet young moon with her attendant, the evening star.

As we passed Elm street we noticed two figures standing by the sea-wall, the silhouettes sharply defined against the pale background. And what was it in the pose of that proud, upturned head that made the Duke start in surprise?

*   *   *   *   *   *

When we reached home we found the flat deserted. The hammock in the library swung gently in the breeze; the flowers in the jardiniere yielded their spiciest fragrance to the evening dews; the lamp shed its rosy light softly on the pretty tea-table, and touched with brightness the branches of apple blossoms that filled the fireless grate, but all was mute; there was no sign.

The Duke sighed, and stooping, picked from among the snowy petals that had fallen to the hearth, the crushed semblance of a little blue butterfly.

www.ingramcontent.com/pod-product-compliance
Lightning Source LLC
Chambersburg PA
CBHW020234030726
47497CB00009B/3087